PRINCIPAL'S OFFICE

THE PRINCIPAL'S UNDERWEAR IS MISSING

Written and illustrated by

HOLLY KOWITT

SQUARE
FISH

Feiwel and Friends
New York

SQUARE FISH

An imprint of Macmillan Publishing Group, LLC
175 Fifth Avenue
New York, NY 10010
mackids.com

Square Fish and the Square Fish logo are trademarks of Macmillan and
are used by Feiwel and Friends under license from Macmillan.

Our books may be purchased in bulk for promotional, educational, or business
use. Please contact your local bookseller or the Macmillan Corporate and
Premium Sales Department at (800) 221-7945 ext. 5442 or by e-mail at
MacmillanSpecialMarkets@macmillan.com.

Library of Congress Cataloging-in-Publication Data is available.

ISBN 9781250158628 (paperback)   ISBN 9781250091338 (ebook)

Originally published in the United States by Feiwel and Friends
First Square Fish edition, 2018
Book designed by Véronique Lefèvre Sweet
Square Fish logo designed by Filomena Tuosto

1   3   5   7   9   10   8   6   4   2

AR: 3.8

For David Manis
Greatest. Husband. Ever.

Chapter 1

Oh no. No, no, no, *no*. Not her. Please, God. *NOT HER!*
Anyone but her.

Five feet away from me, the most beautiful, popular
girl in school howled in pain. Sloan "Selfie" St. Clair,
the undisputed Queen of Cool, Goddess of Eighth
Grade, was on the gym floor, writhing in agony—

Because of me. A lowly sixth grader.

Her   Me

"Owwwwwwwwww. Oooooh. Uggghhhhhhh." She clutched her arm like I'd blown it off with a hand grenade. Her friends looked on in distress, and the gym teacher, Ms. Doyle, swooped in like a giant bird.

"Stay calm! Stay calm!" the teacher shouted. "Give us some SPACE, people!"

The girls around me gasped and looked nervous, like they could somehow be blamed for it, too.

I replayed the past two minutes in my head. We'd been playing volleyball, and a gym full of girls were yelling, "C'mon, Birnbaum! Hit a decent serve for once!" Out of the corner of my eye, I saw some Beautiful People—eighth graders—in the bleachers. What were *they* doing in our gym class?

I didn't need the distraction. Besides being lousy at sports, I was somewhere between Misfit and

Mathlete on the food chain. I gripped the ball in my sweaty hand. *Don't. Be. A. Total. Dork.*

My stomach tensed as I wound up and—*THOOMP!*—whacked the ball as hard as I could. It veered sideways, hit an overhead light, and shot straight down. That was when I heard the scream.

"OWWWWWWWWWW!" Selfie wailed again, jolting me back to the present. She was on her back, clutching her arm and screaming. Someone whispered, "The ball hit Selfie, and she fell and hurt her arm! *That* girl did it." I just stood there with my mouth open.

Stupid, stupid, stupid. Of all people to clobber, why did it have to be an eighth-grade fashion icon who looked like she'd walked off the cover of *Teen Vogue*? The wild child who wore sunglasses inside and carried a jumbo coffee cup, Hollywood starlet-style, as if she'd been up too late the night before? Selfie had gotten her nickname from the pics she always took of herself: at a movie premiere, on the Tilt-A-Whirl, at a swim-up snack bar in Cancún.

Everyone had heard about . . .

Her legendary parties 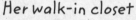 Her walk-in closet

Her summer camp
in Switzerland

The room in her mansion
just for gift wrapping

Other rumors swirled around, too: She was offered a modeling contract. She had inspired a brand of blue jeans. She was dating a high school guy.

"You're in BIG trouble." Another popular girl, Roxxi Barron, wagged her finger at me. "Hitting an eighth grader. Now her arm's probably broken." She looked me up and down, taking in my untamed hair and no-name gym shoes. "Who *are* you, anyway?"

"Nobody," I mumbled.

Who was I? An easy-to-ignore sixth grader at James A. Garfield Middle School—short and freckled, with red glasses, a flat chest, and a closet that looked like the sale rack at Value Village. Killing it in Model UN wasn't exactly the path to popularity.

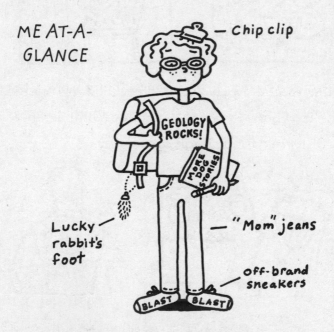

ME AT-A-GLANCE

— Chip clip

GEOLOGY ROCKS!

MORE DOG STORIES

Lucky rabbit's foot

— "Mom" jeans

off-brand sneakers

BLAST   BLAST

Name: Becca Birnbaum
Occupation: sixth grader

Profile: smart, organized, invisible
Bra size: AAAA
Least likely to say: "It's so hard being head
                    cheerleader (sigh)."

Ms. Doyle was still crouched next to Selfie as the girl's sobs filled the gym. Taking a deep breath, I stepped forward to apologize. "STAY BACK!" Doyle shouted, holding up her hand like a policeman.

Like a frightened mouse, I obeyed. There was nothing to do but stand there awkwardly. Roxxi kept shooting me dirty looks, as if the injury were a personal insult to *all* gorgeous, popular eighth graders.

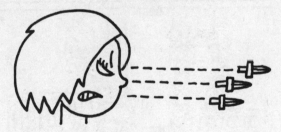

"CLEAR THE WAY! CLEAR THE WAY!" Two uniformed ambulance guys burst through the gym doors, wheeling a stretcher. People looked shocked, panicked, and secretly thrilled. Nothing this exciting had ever happened in gym.

"You okay?" My best friend, Rosa Hadid, squeezed my arm. Her dark eyes locked onto mine, worried.

I shook my head.

"Try not to freak out." She lowered her voice. "Maybe it's not as bad as it looks."

The ambulance guys surrounded Selfie, poking, prodding, and asking questions. Her moans continued. Finally, one of them pulled out a walkie-talkie. "Possible right-side proximal to the scapula," he said. "Rush the bus to Parkside."

The hospital? *Oh, God.*

I tried to picture her there.

My stomach churned. Maiming the most popular girl in school was *not* the best game plan. At Garfield, it didn't take much to get labeled radioactive. A roll of the eyes, a sarcastic giggle, a slide away from you on the school bus—any of these, done by the right person, could seal your fate for the next few years.

"What was the glam crowd even *doing* here?" I whispered to Rosa as the ambulance guys lifted Selfie onto a stretcher.

"Measuring the gym for Fall Frolic." Rosa rolled her eyes. She disapproved of dances, pep rallies, or any event that involved cheesy themes and crepe paper.

The ambulance guys strapped Selfie in. Suddenly, they were flying across the gym. "COMING THROUGHHHHHHH!"

Her friends trailed behind, looking upset as the gurney crashed through the double doors. Roxxi glared back at me.

"You're *dead meat*," she hissed.

I believed her.

Chapter 2

The next day, I dreaded running into Selfie. *Please, please let her be all better!* Then I saw her in the cafeteria.

Crud!

The cast was huge. Just seeing it made me feel even worse. After she was rushed to the hospital, I cursed myself for not getting through to apologize. Now she was right across the room.

Unfortunately, so were all her friends. Talk about *intimidating.*

From my perch at the Geeks and Bookworms table, I could see her talking to popular A-list jocks like Zach Pirotta and "Six-Pack" Feldman, guys who rolled down the halls with lazy confidence. Selfie's girlfriends were there, too—D'Nise Cousins, Vivienne Ling, Margaux Frost, and Roxxi Barron—the royalty of our school. Plus Chaz Green, a guy who hung out with the girls. They traveled together like a bored, beautiful military brigade, marching through school, undefeated.

No way was I going over there. I was sitting with Rosa and our friend Prezbo. I ducked my head and sort of hid behind them.

"Go talk to her *now*," Prezbo said. "This is your big chance."

He was known for strong opinions. Preston Bollinger ("Prezbo") could go on for hours about the Ten Greatest Guitar Solos or most unwatchable Godzilla movie. Although he was impatient with jocks and morons, he knew how to stay on their good side to survive at school. "Infiltrate the system, and then subvert it" was his motto.

"You have to apologize *some*time," Rosa agreed, finishing off a cream-cheese-and-olive sandwich. "Selfie never enters a bathroom with less than ten people, so you're *never* going to find her alone."

I glanced over there again and saw two guys chest-bump. The thought of going up to them made my stomach clench. The "cool" table wasn't exactly welcoming.

Taking a deep breath, I forced my legs to stand. *What's the big deal? You're just going to another part of the cafeteria.* Like most people, though, I knew where I belonged. Skaters didn't sit with glee clubbers; mall rats didn't hang with tech geeks. You didn't cross borders.

I clutched my crumpled lunch bag. That way, if I chickened out, I had something to throw in the garbage. Brilliant, right? Like I always crossed the room to use a less convenient trash can.

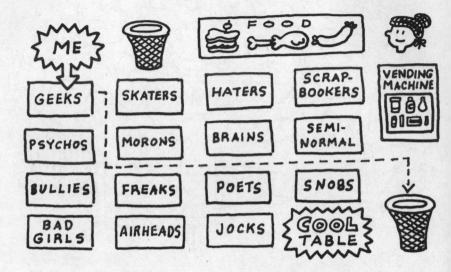

With shaky hands, I approached the table. I could hear them talking.

"Kovac, that is so rude—"

"DE-*NIED!*"

"On sale from Zappos. Seventy-nine dollars plus tax."

No one noticed me.

"Ahem," I said.

They kept right on talking. I knew I wasn't popular but didn't realize I was *actually* invisible. I tried again.

"Um ... hey ... Selfie?"

The Queen Bee was talking to someone and didn't seem to hear. Roxxi jumped up and leaped between us. Like a self-appointed nightclub bouncer, she folded her arms and looked at me through slitted eyes. "What do *you* want?"

I mumbled that I wanted to see Selfie.

"Selfie!?" Roxxi sputtered, like I'd just requested an audience with the pope. "You want to talk to *Selfie*?"

Margaux looked up. "Who wants to talk to Selfie?"

Oh, *brother*. "I'm just trying—"

Everyone at the table turned around, alarmed at the security breach. Unaware, Selfie and Vivienne were still gabbing away.

"I . . . I need to tell her something," I said.

"She can't be disturbed." Roxxi folded her arms.

Selfie chattered on. I heard the words *wedge heel* and *peep-toe*. Vivienne made a point about ankle straps. *Not exactly a conference on world hunger.*

"Go back to chess team, or whatever," Roxxi said. "We'll give her the message." Her friends cracked up.

Their laughter burned my throat. "I want to tell her myself."

Roxxi, Margaux, D'Nise, and Chaz exchanged a look that said, *Can you believe this sixth grader?* But I didn't care. I hadn't dragged myself all the way here just to be swatted away like a mosquito.

Suddenly, Selfie got to her feet. With her good arm, she hoisted up a fancy leather purse on a gold chain. *Oh no!* She was leaving—and I hadn't gotten to apologize!

"Selfie!" I called. *"Selfie!"*

Roxxi looked furious—and astonished. But this time, I wasn't giving up.

"SELFIEEEEEEE!!!" I yelled.

The cafeteria went silent.

Selfie turned toward me, slowly. Everyone watched as the Queen Bee approached me, with her nose-up, runway model's way of walking. Suddenly, we were face-to-face!

"I'm, uh . . ." My voice trailed off. Now that I had her attention, I didn't know what to say. Selfie blinked and tilted her head.

"She's the one who bonked you." Roxxi's voice was flat.

"I'm, really, um . . ." My eyes were glued to the floor. "SorryboutwhathappenedletmeknowifIcanhelp."

Selfie stared at me a second. When she opened her mouth to speak, my hands started to shake. *This was it!* The moment I'd been dreading! Everyone held their breath.

And then, a totally weird thing happened.

A girl ran up and shoved a phone in Selfie's face. The Queen Bee looked at it and screamed—a cry of pain so raw I got chills down my back. Everyone started whispering. What the heck was going on?

A second later, D'Nise, Vivienne, Chaz, and Margaux surrounded her like a SWAT team for the super popular. They made soothing sounds, stroking her hair and handing her gum, lip gloss, and wet wipes. Someone threw an EIGHTH-GRADE SOCCER windbreaker over her shoulders.

They whisked her away, as if to a waiting helicopter. Stranded at the empty table, I stood there stupidly. Then Roxxi came over to me.

"Listen, sixth grader." She poked my chest. "You lucked out today."

I did?

"Selfie's in the middle of a *major* crisis."

"Oh. Wow. Uh—"

"Don't ask what it is, cuz it's *top secret*," Roxxi cut me off, and then waited. When I didn't press for details, she cleared her throat. "*No one* needs to know."

"Okay." I shrugged.

"Cuz it would, like, *totally* devastate her."

Ha! I was dying to find out, but it was more fun to deny Roxxi the chance to tell me. "I understand," I said calmly.

Roxxi's eyes turned angry. "Listen, Diptard, you need to get something straight! Selfie didn't have time to deal with you, cuz there was this *disaster*, and she totally *freaked*. But when she sees you again?" She whistled. "*Total* smackdown."

Overhearing us, Jenna Dempsey, a semipopular seventh grader, came over and nodded. "*I* wouldn't want to get on her bad side."

"Remember Maya Wagner?" another girl piped up. "After Selfie dissed her, she started homeschooling."

Pretty soon, a crowd had gathered. Everyone had a story:

"Her dad owns half the city—"

"She's gotten *teachers* fired!"

"They rescheduled graduation so she could go to the World Cup!"

Now I was sweating through my T-shirt. These rumors were really getting to me. What next—they changed daylight saving time so Selfie could sleep late?

Just how freakin' powerful is she?

"This is ridiculous!" I burst out, exasperated. "No one is THAT big a deal! What the heck am I supposed to do? TRANSFER????"

Silence. My words hung in the air, uncontradicted, while everyone looked at the floor, their nails, or the ceiling tiles.

Chapter 3

For the next twenty-four hours, my mission was: Stay Away From Selfie. Luckily, most of her hangouts weren't that hard to avoid:

The only problem was the bathroom. The Beautiful People assembled there when they needed to apply lip liner, gossip, or discuss last weekend's Hawaiian luau. Having it off-limits all day wasn't easy.

On the other hand, the Mix 'N' Math picnic seemed like a secure location. So when the last bell rang, I bounced down the hall and headed to the East Courtyard.

But passing by the Multi-Purpose Room, I heard a gasp.

"UMMGH! UNH! UPF!"

I ran inside. Underneath a spray-painted sign that said CLOTHING-DRIVE DONATIONS, a rack of coats had fallen over, pinning someone under it. Frantically, I started clearing away wool and fleece. Finally, a hand appeared—*yes!* The hand led to an arm; the arm led to a cast.

A cast?

It was SELFIE! *Crud!*

I cleared away a raincoat, and our eyes met. "Oh!" She sat up. "You're the one who . . ."

Run! Go! NOW!

"It was an accident!" I shouted. "I *said* I was sorry. For God's sake, can't you just LET IT GO?"

Selfie stared at me.

"You think I *wanted* to mangle the most popular girl in school?" I yelled. "You think I *wanted* to commit social suicide? That I woke up one day and decided to . . . to . . ."

She blinked.

CRUD! What was I doing, yelling at the Queen Bee? I shut up and waited for the ax to fall.

She blinked again.

Say something, I begged silently. Her mouth twisted, like she was deciding how to kill me. Firing squad? Shark tank? My head was about to explode. *Just get it over with!*

Finally, she gave a little shrug.

"Don't worry about it."

Huh?

"I've moved on. Totes. No biggie." And then she smiled. A big, dazzling, Crest Whitestrip smile.

My jaw dropped.

"Obvi, you didn't mean to. It was a rando accident." Selfie wiggled the cast. "This thing's a drag, but people keep bringing me candy and carrying my books. Not too shabs. Twizzler?"

Whooooa!

Was this the same hotshot eighth grader who ruled the school and scared us all to death?

Still in shock, I pulled up the clothing rack and helped Selfie shake off the last few coats. She sank into a chair and motioned for me to join her. I sat down and took a licorice stick, amazed. *In what world do super-popular Cool People you've injured turn out to be friendly?*

Not at all
what I was
picturing

"Sorry I bolted after you apologized the other day," Selfie said. "An embarrassing pic of me and my secret crush just went viral. *Major* traumarama." She showed me her phone.

"I wasn't up for going public yet. Things with Paolo and me are very delicate right now," she said. "You know that stage where he lends you his sweatshirt and eats fries off your plate but won't ask you on a non-group date?"

"Sure," I lied. *Boy, do I have a lot to learn.*

"Hand me a brush?" She pointed to her purse. "My hair looks like dog barf."

I reached into the overflowing bag on the table next to me. As I looked for a brush, other things spilled out:

"What's this?" I pointed to a laminated card.

"Fake ID."

Fascinating. It was like studying artifacts from some exotic tribe. Could our lives be any more different?

My hand plunged into the purse again and found the brush tangled in the straps of a bikini. I pulled it out and handed it to her, and she started brushing forcefully. "Now I have to deal with this clothing drive," she said, looking around. "What a maj disaster."

"It *is* pretty messy," I agreed.

"Reindeer sweaters! *Star Wars* pajamas! Tuxedo T-shirts!"

Oh. It wasn't the chaos that bothered her; it was the bad taste.

"I promised to sort through donations." She sighed. "But Fashion Club meets in fifteen, and I'll never get through 'em all."

"Gosh, let me help." The math picnic could wait. "It would make me feel a *little* less guilty."

"Thanks, um . . ." Selfie blushed. "What's your name?"

"Becca. Becca Birnbaum."

As we sorted clothes into piles, Selfie had an opinion about every belt, turtleneck, and down vest. The death of various fashion trends was announced. Mittens were rejected for being "too last year." Sometimes she acted like she was handling nuclear waste.

PING! Selfie picked up her phone. As she glanced at the screen, her face darkened. "Uh-*oh*."

"What?"

"Aaaaagh!" She picked up a rain boot and hurled it across the room, muttering a French swear word.

"Tell me!" I begged.

Selfie sat down and buried her head in her hands. "I got a D minus on my algebra test." Her voice came out in a sob. "Lewison called my mom."

"Oh, boy."

"It's not just algebra." Tears rolled down her face. "It's *everything*. My mom's bugging me to hang out with Bentley—her friend's son—a brainiac who's not too chill. And Roxxi's been acting psycho since I got this injury. I think she's actually jealous of the attention! Crazy, right?"

"Isn't Roxxi your good friend . . . ?" I was confused.

"Yeah." Her voice was bitter. "The kind of friend who posts an insta of you with flat hair and flirts with your boyfriend."

Aha. Now I saw the two of them in a different light—rivals, not BFFs.

"I don't have an art project to hand in," she continued. "My mom wants me home ASAP—but Fashion Club's in ten minutes, and I'm prez! My shopping bag got taken away cuz I was talking in class; now the principal's got it." She pointed to her feet. "And look what happened to my new high-heeled sneaks! They

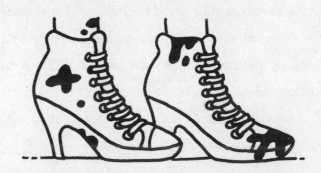

got trashed when I spray-painted the clothing-drive sign." Seeing her feet again led to fresh sobs. "Why am I telling you all this?"

I knew why. I was so out of her orbit it didn't matter. It was like confiding to a goldfish.

"Don't worry," I said. "We can figure something out." The *we* just slipped out.

"Maybe you're right." She wiped her eyes. "I just have to come up with a plan! And that's what I'm *great* at. Let's see . . . invent a jet ski accident? Family emergency? My cousin needs my kidney?"

Think, I told myself. Staring at the floor, I felt my mind go blank. Then I saw her paint-splattered shoes. "Huh."

"What?"

"Maybe you could—" *No, that's crazy.* "Never mind."

"WHAT?"

I took a deep breath. Did I dare? "Okay, well, here's another idea. Have the brainiac tutor you in math. Flatter Roxxi by asking her to run Fashion Club today—then you can go deal with your mom. Put *more* spray paint on your sneakers, and hand them in as your art project. And I'll go to the principal and pick up your shopping bag." I shrugged. "Just a thought."

Selfie stared at me.

I gulped, feeling uncomfortable. Had I offended the queen?

Silence.

"*More* paint on my sneakers? That's *ridic.*" But she was sitting up straighter. And eyeing me carefully, as if seeing me for the first time.

Suddenly, the door banged open. "More clothes!" Chaz Green, looking crisp in a striped button-down shirt, dumped two bags on the floor. "Fur boots from Mandy Southern, and nerdy baseball hats from Felix Needleman. As if anyone would want . . ." When he saw me, he stopped mid-sentence, shocked.

There was an awkward silence. According to the Unwritten Rules, the two of us didn't talk to each other. He belonged to the popular crowd but hung around the girls, not the jocks. I often saw him with three or four of them, straightening a collar, tying a scarf, or whispering in someone's ear. I suddenly saw myself through his eyes.

"*You're* not in Fashion Club," he said.

Selfie opened her mouth and closed it, as if changing her mind. Then she lifted her chin. "Yes, she is."

WHAT?

Chaz's eyes bulged. "But—!"

Selfie tossed her hair back with fierce confidence. The girl who'd been crying five minutes ago transformed back into the aloof Queen of Cool. Selfie swung a tanned arm around my shoulder.

"She's with me."

Chapter 4

"So you two are, like, FRIENDS now?" Rosa's voice rose in disbelief. "Last I knew, you were avoiding bathrooms so you wouldn't run into her." We were at our lockers, gathering up our things. My pal Rosa was the opposite of Selfie—a total tomboy. She stuffed the essentials into her backpack: drumsticks, catcher's mitt, paintball shirt. She was ready.

"Selfie's not my friend," I said quickly. Saying her name gave me a weird thrill. "I just said I'd do her a favor."

"A favor?" Prezbo snorted. "What could you do for *her*?"

His snort annoyed me. I was super organized and paid attention to stuff. When we watched movies, I always figured out who the murderer was. Why couldn't I help?

"Selfie wants me to go to the principal's office and pick up her shopping bag," I said. "She was talking in class, so the teacher confiscated it and took it to Dr. Valentine. No big deal." I didn't say she'd been showing off her new glitter socks from Sandstrom's.

"You're going to Valentine's office? Yikes." Prezbo pretended to shudder. Everyone was scared of her. "Do you have a death wish?"

"Forget that," said Rosa. "The real question is, why are you doing chores for an eighth grader? Are you her maid or something?" *Geez!* They were interrogating me like a criminal on *Law & Order*.

I had to phrase this the right way. "I'm just trying to help out, after the injury and all. Her life seems pretty crazy."

"Sounds like you feel sorry for her." Rosa said it like an accusation. "But *why*? She's gorgeous, popular, and loaded. Her earrings probably cost more than your house."

"Not *sorry*, exactly . . ." I couldn't put my feelings about Selfie into words. Yes, she was self-absorbed and kind of ridiculous. But she'd been nice to me, and I liked helping her out. She had access to things I knew nothing about—boys, foreign countries, high school. I felt like I'd been given an older sister for an hour.

"What's in it for you?" asked Prezbo, stuffing books into his backpack.

"I don't know." I didn't want to sound starstruck. Rosa and Prezbo and I had always laughed at the cool crowd, with their spirit rallies and winter beach parties and mother-daughter fashion shows. We made fun of the high-fiving jocks and the girls who loved them.

THUMP
THUMP
THUMP...

"Selfie is . . ." I took another stab at explaining it. "Just seeing what was in her purse was amazing.

It's like she's on another planet. I felt like a spy or something."

I fingered a piece of fancy Swiss chocolate she'd given me, which I'd held on to like it was a moon rock.

"Besides," I added. "I kind of like her."

Stunned silence.

"Huh." A wave of surprise passed over Rosa's face, but then she smiled. "Okay, cool. *I* think she sounds like a flake. But of course, I want to hear every detail." I was grateful. The ice was broken—a little.

Prezbo checked his watch. "I've got to get out of here. I'm reviewing *Alien Gang Wars IV,* and Rob'll squawk if I'm late." Rob Robson was the anchor for the school's *Action News,* where Prezbo was the video game critic.

"I should go." I motioned toward the principal's office.

"Me too. Band practice." Rosa punched my shoulder. "Good luck."

Good luck? It wasn't something to be nervous about. All I had to do was go to the principal's office, grab the confiscated shopping bag, and return it to Selfie. Pick it up, bring it back, *done.*

How hard could that be?

• • • • •

"I'll get the Box." Mr. Maslon, the principal's secretary, cut me off when I explained what I was there for. He pulled earbuds out of his ears and reached under his desk for an overflowing cardboard container. I guess Selfie wasn't the only one who'd had her stuff taken away.

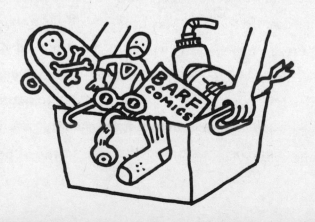

"Nerf football. Fake vomit. Everything bagel." Maslon recited the list in a weary voice. "And that's just from *today*." He was a balding, slight man who always seemed mildly annoyed.

I sorted through the box and shook my head. "Um, I'm looking for a shopping bag."

He frowned. "Bigger items are kept in the office. I hate to disturb Dr. Valentine. . . ." He glanced at the door marked PRINCIPAL and tapped a pencil on his desk. "Is it urgent?"

"Well . . ." I didn't want to flub this. "Yes. I do need that bag. Sorry, can I just run in and . . . ?"

He sighed heavily and pressed a button on the phone. "Dr. Valentine? Student here to retrieve confiscated item."

"Good luck." He raised his eyebrows.

Why do people keep saying that?

I took a deep breath. How tough *was* Dr. Valentine, anyway? I'd never met her personally, but I'd heard stories: She had blocked a kid's graduation because of an overdue library book. She had expelled someone for littering. The "swear jar" on her desk had paid for a vacation to Disney World. Kids were scared of her.

VALENTINE AT-A-GLANCE

Name: Dr. Jasmine Valentine
Occupation: principal
Reputation: tough, well-dressed
Hobby: country-western line dancing
Pet peeve: private parts drawn on textbooks
Quote: "What is it this time, Franklin?
　　　　Tardiness? Littering? Under-the-
　　　　desk gum wads?"

I'd never been to her office before, and I felt a tingle of anticipation. Maslon nodded for me to go on in. All the things I'd heard about were there:

Dr. Valentine looked up from her computer, peering at me over half-glasses. Up close, she was dazzling—a tall, glossy-haired woman dressed in a maroon silk shirt and gray suit, smelling of fruity perfume. A silver brooch sparkled on the lapel of her jacket. Her lips and fingernails were the same deep red. Without thinking, I tucked in my shirt.

"I'm here to pick up Sloan St. Clair's shopping bag," I said, not daring to call her "Selfie." Valentine probably disapproved of nicknames. On the floor, I spotted a shiny white shopping bag with the familiar logo. *Bingo.*

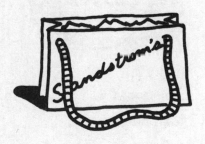

"Sloan St. Clair," Valentine repeated, leaning back in her chair. She smiled and gestured for me to sit down.

I nodded.

"Why didn't she come herself?" Valentine frowned.

"She had a meeting."

"And you are . . . ?" Valentine tapped a pen on the desk.

"Becca. Her, uh, friend."

"*You're* a friend of Ms. St. Clair?" Valentine's voice rose. Even *she* could see how unlikely that was. I nodded uncertainly.

The vibe in the room was *very* weird. Valentine stood up and folded her arms.

"Tell me something, Ms.—"

"Birnbaum," I whispered, suddenly scared.

"*Birnbaum.*" Valentine walked around the desk with excruciating slowness. When she reached my chair, she stopped and sat on the edge of her desk.

Our eyes were level. "Your 'friend' is well-known to this office. Are you"—her tone was almost casual—"a troublemaker, too?"

WHAT?

"ME!? No!" I sputtered, panicked. "I'm ... ask anyone! I've never—I mean, I always—" Boy, did she have the wrong impression.

Dr. Valentine waited.

"I get straight As! I won the Current Events Baton! I go to biology camp! I—" The words didn't come fast enough.

"Mmm-hmm. Mmm-hmm. So let me ask." Valentine stroked her chin. "Why do you *associate* with troublemakers?"

"Uhhh . . ." *Crud!* I finally got the principal's attention, and it wasn't for winning the Junior Knowledge Bowl but for being friends with a delinquent. *Who I'm not even friends with!*

Getting on Valentine's bad side would be a *very* bad move. You needed her approval to do *anything* at school—start a club, miss a class, take high school-level French.

"Listen, Dr. Valentine . . ." My heart was pounding. "I'm *not* involved. Truth is, I barely know Selfie." In five seconds, I'd demoted her from BFF to stranger.

"She asked me to do her a favor; that's all. So I'll just take her bag and—" I started to get up.

"Not so fast." Valentine pointed to my chair, smiling again. "Sit down, Ms. Birnbaum."

"But—"

"Sit down."

My butt hit the seat.

"I'd like to ask you something else." Dr. Valentine dropped her smile. "Do you think students at this school should flout the rules? Have sushi delivered for lunch and wear high heels to gym? Use the bathroom as their own personal wellness spa?"

"Um . . ." *Wow.*

"Skip school to see an R-rated movie? Show up tardy because of last night's 'après-ski' party?" Her eyes narrowed. *"Do you think that's acceptable?"*

For a second, I was too astonished to speak.

"DO YOU?" Valentine's voice rose.

How did *I* end up getting lectured for stuff I'd never done or even dreamed of? *Sushi delivery?!*

I finally caught my breath. "NOOO!!" Now I couldn't get words out fast enough. "That's—that's *awful!* Totally out of line!"

Valentine edged closer to me. "*Are you sure*, Ms. Birnbaum? Perhaps you share Ms. St. Clair's point of view—'rules don't apply to me.' So I need to hear you can tell right from wrong. I need to hear *you know better than that*. Do we understand each other?"

Valentine's eyes were blazing. How many students had sat in this seat, getting yelled at for graffiti tags, sass-backs, school bus moonings, swirlies, slam books, cherry bombs, and faked flus? She whipped off her glasses and grabbed the armrests of my chair. I shrank back, terrified.

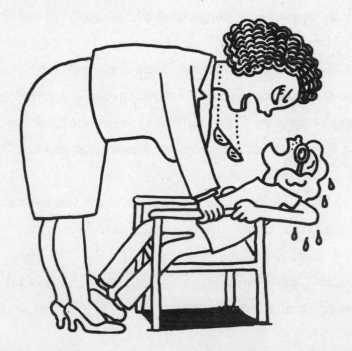

"Well, Miss Birnbaum?" she thundered.

"YES!" I gasped. "That stuff is WRONG! Absolutely!"

"*That's* what I want to hear." Valentine sighed and walked back behind her desk in a queenly way. She pointed at me and nodded. "You may take the bag."

Finally! I leaped up and grabbed the silk rope handles.

"When you see Ms. St. Clair, will you give her a message?" Valentine sat down and put on her glasses. She leaned across the desk, motioning for me to come closer.

"A message for Selfie?" I felt an uneasy quiver in my stomach. I sensed it wasn't going to be "You won the Junior Science Talent Search!"

"Tell your friend . . ." Valentine's voice got softer. "She better get her act together. I'm *serious.* Because if she has one more slipup, and I mean *one more . . .*"

I held my breath.

"You know what she's looking at?" she whispered.

No! Tell me!

"SUSPENSION."

The word dropped like a bomb. *Suspension.* It had a mesmerizing quality, a fate so dreaded and mysterious it destroyed all competition for the Worst Thing That Could Happen. What would become of the Queen Bee?

I burst out of the room. *Get the bag to Selfie*, my brain screamed as I ran down the hall. That was when I made my Tragic Mistake. I was so eager to deliver the bag . . .

I never looked inside.

Chapter 5

Five pairs of eyes stared as I ran up to Selfie. The queen's entourage stood together in the hall, like a well-dressed human fortress. They were all there: D'Nise Cousins, Vivienne Ling, Margaux Frost, Roxxi Barron, Chaz Green. A hiss of surprise ran through the group as I tapped Selfie on the shoulder. The last time I had approached her and the "cool" clan, I felt sick with fear and dread. Was it only twenty-four hours ago? Now it felt totally different.

This time, I have something she wants.

"Oh!" Selfie squealed, grabbing the silk rope handles. "You ROCK!"

Roxxi's eyes burned as Selfie stuffed the shiny bag into her enormous purse and gave off squeals of delight. D'Nise, Selfie's best friend, arched an eyebrow at my hemmed jeans and babyish T-shirt. I saw her exchange an impatient glance with Chaz that said, *Why is this twerp still hanging around?*

"No prob," I shot back in Selfie-lingo. I didn't mention Valentine had almost bitten my head off.

"That's *amaze*," Selfie went on gratefully. "Principal's, like, way harsh with me; I don't know why. It's like that *every time* I'm sent to her office!"

I coughed. Her friends looked increasingly un-
happy as Selfie bubbled over in appreciation. I could
tell what they were thinking.

"S'nothing." I waved my hand, enjoying her friends'
scowls.

Selfie reached into her purse to pull out a brush,
an awkward move with her arm in a sling. Her purse
tumbled to the floor, scattering makeup brushes,
Swiss chocolate bars, concert tickets, and foreign
money. "Oops!"

"I GOT THIS!!!" six people yelled.

I dived for it, too, but D'Nise beat us all. With
manicured hands, she swept up jeweled barrettes, a

Chinese fan, and an Air France sleep mask. D'Nise was Selfie's "bestie," the one who knew her locker combination by heart and could back up an alibi after a late-night yacht party. D'Nise was a major diva herself, with a drop-dead wardrobe and serious bling.

Not to be outdone by D'Nise, Chaz moved in to brush off Selfie's purse while Vivienne untangled the strap. Margaux handed her a tube of lotion and a Smartwater. The message was clear: *Selfie doesn't need you, dweeb.*

But a rogue pot of lip gloss was still rolling lazily across the floor. I scooped it up and handed it to her.

"Don't forget . . ." I smiled sweetly.

"Thanks, Becca." Selfie's smile was dazzling. "You're fab."

They all glared. God, this was fun.

. . . • . .

Rosa and I were parked in my family's den, allegedly studying but really hate-watching *Eighth-Grade Bucket List* and *Totally Trevor!* on the Teen Channel. The shows played on mute as I described Selfie's friends falling over one another to hand her tubes of pomegranate-and-sage hand cream.

"Sheesh." Rosa snorted. She leaned down to pet her dog, Rascal, a sleepy mutt who went everywhere with her. Rosa was a tomboy and comics freak, so the only makeup she ever used was Wonder Woman lip balm. She also refused to wear purses, hair accessories, and the color pink. This sometimes upset her traditional Lebanese parents, who wanted her to wear skirts and take ballet.

"I know, right?" I shook my head.

Rosa picked up her drumsticks and started a solo on her *Gateway to Algebra* book. "Look, you did her a favor—good. Obligation over! You can go back to normal life."

Normal life. I thought about my upcoming week and felt my chest sink.

"Yeah." I tried to sound relieved, but inside, I was sad. My collision with Selfie World had ended. I'd done her a favor and tried to make up for injuring her. Future contact would be limited to airy hellos in the hall.

"Hey, you okay?" Rosa's dark eyes moved over me. "I thought you'd just be grateful to get out of that mess in one piece."

"Totally." I nodded, appreciating Rosa's reminder. I was lucky just to survive it. Getting a peek into that older, exotic world was just a crazy bonus—not the beginning of something real. So what if Selfie and I had shared a few moments together? Wanting more was greedy.

Better to spend time with good friends like Rosa and Prezbo, who I genuinely hit it off with. *Friends my age* who did well in school but didn't take themselves too seriously. Pals who tolerated each other's weird interests—Prezbo's homemade YouTube movies, Rosa's obsession with *Consumer Reports* magazine, my crazy notebook doodles. We saw the world the same way.

Rosa's drumming grew more furious. "I'm done studying," she announced. She was so smart she zipped through assignments. "Let's *do* something. Library? Kick the can? Nature's Bounty for free samples?"

"Um . . ."

"*King's Road*?" she continued. Our favorite British spy show from the sixties. The heroes were stylish and dry and used wit to solve crimes. They had bullet-proof bowler hats and an umbrella that turned into a sword.

"S'almost dinner, so I better . . ."

THUD! Something hit the sliding glass door of the den, and then we heard the clang of metal on con-crete. Rosa dropped her drumsticks. "ARF-R-RF!" howled Rascal, rousing himself. Had a car plowed into my house? We looked at each other, startled. What in the ...?

THUMP! THUMP! THUMP! Someone was pounding on the glass. I ran to the sliding door.

"BECCAAAAAA! BECCAAAAA!!!!"

Whose voice was that? I threw back the curtain and gasped. *Holy crud!*

"*SELFIE?*"

No freakin' way.

"Open up!! EMERGENCY!"

I slid the door open and saw Selfie pull her purse out of a—*was that a golf cart???*

The overturned vehicle lay on its side on the patio, its roof shattered. She swept into the room and leaned against the wall. "Traffic was insane," she said between big gasps of breath. "So much road rage!"

I could only imagine....

"Where'd you get—"

"I 'borrowed' it from the country club." She made a guilty face. "It was an emergency!"

She sure had a lot of emergencies.

Good thing my mom worked at the library today, or she'd be freaking out. Rascal kept yapping at the top of his lungs, while Selfie tossed her purse across the room with her free arm. Rosa ducked and yelled, "Hey! Watch it!"

"OHHH! I didn't even see you there!" Selfie's hand flew over her mouth as the purse hit the wall. She rubbed her forehead. "So sorry. This day has been *cray*."

Rosa just stared.

"I—I better get going," she said, gathering up her books in a trance. Even Rosa, usually absurdly confident, seemed intimidated. Her face said, *What the heck is she doing here?* Mine said, *No freakin' idea.*

"You don't have to go," I said. "Seriously."

"Totes!" Selfie nodded vigorously. "I didn't mean to bust things up. But this is kind of a 911-type situation."

Somehow, I was skeptical. "What do you mean?"

"I'll spill, but first I need provisions." Selfie kicked off high-heeled stiletto sandals and collapsed dramatically onto the sofa. She closed her eyes. "I'd KILL for lavender bubble tea."

"Sorry, we just have OJ and—"

"JOKE! LaCroix water's fine."

We didn't have that, either. Rosa started for the door again. Selfie opened her eyes and pointed to Rosa's messenger bag. "Sick purse."

"What?" Rosa looked startled.

"Military chic." Selfie gave a thumbs-up. "Cool."

"Oh." Rosa looked down at her bag, confused.

Had two more different people ever been in a room together?

When Selfie started in on her sneakers, Rosa bolted. "Killer low-tops!" Selfie called after her. Rosa looked at me with raised eyebrows as she pulled Rascal through the sliding door. Turning to Selfie, I felt a wave of impatience, even though I was also sort of thrilled. What was the big "emergency"?

Broken mascara wand?　　Wobbly high heel?　　Nail polish shortage?

I handed Selfie a glass of seltzer, which she drank with long, theatrical gulps. She was really playing this to the hilt. This time, I wasn't falling for it. "So what's this Major Catastrophe?" I joked gently, trying to lighten the mood. "That made you hightail it over in a stolen vehicle?"

But I didn't get the expected laugh.

Instead, she bit her lip, looking pale, nauseated, and really strange.

"Listen, Becca." Selfie's eyes were desperate. "That bag from the principal. *Did you open it?*"

I shook my head.

"In that case," Selfie said quietly, "you better sit down."

- - ● - -

We relocated to my bedroom for privacy, in case one of my parents came home early. I'd always liked my cozy little nest, with its slanted ceiling, board games, and bulging bookshelves. Seeing it now through Selfie's eyes, though, I thought it looked hopelessly childish. Everything in it suddenly embarrassed me.

Ceramic horses

Ballerina clock

Dolls of many countries

Jar full o' bugs

But Selfie didn't react. She threw herself down on the patchwork quilt and buried her head in my pillow. I settled in the rocking chair, displacing two stuffed animals. *If she'd told me she was coming, I could've hidden this stuff.*

"Okay." When she wasn't looking, I kicked a bunny slipper under the bed. "Spill."

Selfie moaned.

"The *bag*, Selfie." I tugged the quilt. "What was in it?"

Selfie sat up and looked at me intensely. "You sure you're ready for this?"

"Yes."

Selfie took a deep breath. "You picked up my shopping bag from the principal. I opened it on the way to Fashion Club, thinking I'd find my new glitter socks. But inside was a pair of old-school panty hose—not mine, *obvi*. And that wasn't all. Under the panty hose, wrapped in tissue, was . . . was . . ."

"Was . . . ?" I nodded impatiently.

Selfie looked at me head-on. "A bra."

"Bra?"

"Bra."

WHOA!

"Triple D," Selfie added, lips curving into a smile. "Swear to *God*."

My heart jumped. "That's big, right?"

"*Way* big," said Selfie. "Huge. Humongous!"

Huge. Humongous. Triple D. Then it hit me—of course!

WOW.

"You mean it belongs—" I began.

"Who else—"

"But that's CRAZY!" I gasped.

"That's what I'm saying!" Selfie exploded.

We had the principal's bra! The two of us were shrieking, laughing so hard we slid to the floor, clutching our stomachs. "HA HA HA! OH OH OH!" Our throats were raw from screaming. It was too insane: We had the principal's bra! *The principal's bra!* The one who scared us to death, ruined lives with the stroke of a pen, and was the subject of endless fascination, terror, and gossip. The Big Cheese, Top Dog, Punisher in Chief, Dean o' Detention, Val the Impaler, Stalin-in-Cowboy-Boots. And we had her *bra*!

"Well?" I held out my hand. "Fork it over!"

Selfie's laughter stopped abruptly.

"The bra." I wiggled my fingers. "Give it here."

The color drained out of her face. Suddenly, she looked deeply miserable.

"Aw, Selfie." I patted her shoulder awkwardly. She'd been so worried! It was probably a relief to tell someone. "S'okay. Really. I'll return the bag to Valentine tomorrow. *What can she do to us?* This is on her."

Selfie had a very weird look on her face.

"Thanks." She coughed. "But there's one teensy little problem."

"What?"

"I can't find it."

HUH?

"You can't . . ." I blinked. "WHAT?"

"It's missing." Selfie bowed her head.

"Missing," I repeated dumbly. "What do you mean, 'missing'?"

She shook her head. "I don't have it."

"Selfie." I seized her good arm and then let go, remembering who she was. "This is *really, really* important. You didn't . . . you didn't . . . *show* it to anyone else, did you?"

I held my breath.

Tell me you didn't. Tell me you didn't. Tell me—

"Absolutely not," said Selfie.

THANK GOD! PHEW! Relief surged through me.

"Except D'Nise, Margaux, Roxxi, Chaz, Vivienne . . ." Selfie continued.

That's when I knew we were in trouble.

Chapter 6

"Refreshments, ladies?" Reinhardt, Selfie's family chauffeur, turned around when we came to a stoplight. "We have dark chocolate, Brie, Italian soft drinks. . . ." We were in the backseat of a long, fancy luxury car.

"*Danke schön*, Reinhardt," said Selfie, applying color to her lips. "We're good. There'll be snacks at the club."

We were rushing to Sheltering Oaks, Selfie's country club, to track down Fashion Club members. I persuaded her that we should question each one to see if they had any idea where the bra was.

"Can he go any faster?" I whispered to Selfie. "This is an *emergency!*" Now it was my turn to freak out.

"See? You didn't believe me when *I* said it." Selfie smacked her lips together and squinted into a travel mirror.

I barely remembered. Everything before twenty minutes ago was pretty hazy. That was when Selfie dumped the news on me that life, as I knew it, was officially over.

"Can you step it up, Reinhardt?" Selfie tapped him on the back. "We're in a *crazy* hurry."

VROOM! The car lurched forward. Was this really me, riding in a glamorous VIP car? Usually, the chauffeur was my mom, and the "limo," a dented green Honda Civic. Too bad Reinhardt had been driving Selfie's mother earlier, or Selfie wouldn't have had to bust up a golf cart. I guess it never occurred to her to use anything as ordinary as a bike.

"When we get there, who are we looking for?" I asked.

As Selfie rattled off the names, I felt panic rise in my throat. "D'Nise, Margaux, Roxxi, Chaz, Vivienne, Beckett, Jaden, Lisbeth, Clementine . . ." So many people!

"How did you happen to tell them about the . . ." My voice dropped to a whisper. *"You know."*

Selfie steadied her hand as she applied mascara. "Well, they were at Fashion Club when I opened the bag. And I tell them *everything*."

"Uh-huh. Yeah. Sure." I made sympathetic sounds, trying not to reveal how I felt at that moment.

Selfie sighed. "So I was at the meeting, passing the bra around..."

Passing the bra around!

"To give everyone a look..."

Sheesh.

"But we had agenda items like Prom Hair Dos and Don'ts and a report on floral lace-up boots, so we set it aside. Sometime during the meeting, it disappeared. I even went back to search the room. It was right there, and then: *poof!* It was gone."

"You mean—" I was confused.

"Yep. I was bra-napped."

I looked at her.

"In broad daylight."

I felt nauseated. We were in deep, deep trouble—
the kind that got you expelled, transferred, or worse.
In the eyes of Dr. Valentine, I'd be just as guilty as
Selfie, maybe more. After all, the last person seen
with the bag was . . .

Me.

"Selfie . . ." I tried to be gentle, but I was flipping
out. *If the principal gives you her bra by mistake, it's
weird and awkward and mortifying enough. But if, by
some bizarre twist of fate, that happens . . . YOU'D
BETTER. NOT. FREAKIN'. LOSE IT.*

"This is really, really important. Do those people
know . . ." I swallowed. "Who the bra belongs to?"

Selfie nodded.

Noooooo!

"But don't worry." Selfie patted my arm. "Everyone *swore* not to tell."

So avoiding disaster rested on the school's biggest gossips keeping a giant, juicy secret? "Do you, uh, know how BAD this is?" The alarm in my voice even made Reinhardt turn around.

"I don't think you understand, Becca." The Queen Bee sniffed and sat up taller. "*I'm* the victim here."

Oh, boy. I did an inner eye roll as I looked out the window. The car turned into a massive circular driveway, lined with tall trees. We pulled up to a building I'd only glimpsed through iron gates.

Something told me the "cool" crowd would *not* be glad to see me.

At least five jaws dropped when I walked into the country club's Teen Lounge. Roxxi almost choked on her mini taco. "You've *got* to be kidding." She looked like she was about to call security. "Do you even *play* tennis?" she asked.

"Teen Lounge is for eighth grade and older." Vivienne folded her arms. "We could have you kicked out."

"This isn't Insect Club," Chaz said, and everyone giggled.

Wait till I start interrogating them, I thought. *They'll love that.*

Selfie walked up behind me. "She's my guest," she said, putting an arm around my shoulder. Roxxi & Co. were temporarily silenced. Selfie pulled two iced drinks off a waiter's tray and handed me one. "Want to hit the omelet station?" she asked.

Omelet station? I looked around, and sure enough, a man in a chef's hat was flipping frying pans. In another corner, a guy was hand-rolling sushi.

Waiters walked by with sliders. *Whoa!*

"No, Selfie, we don't have time to eat! We've got to question Roxxi and—" I grabbed a chicken satay skewer. "Are they having a party?"

"No, it's always like this."

"Wow." The room was like a teen dream: Food stations. Arcade games. Foosball. Ping-Pong. Pool table. Giant-screen TV. Basketball hoop. Mini putting green. Lava lamps. A deejay working turntables in the corner. Round, plush couches. Photo booth. Popcorn machine. Jukebox. Holy moly!

"Hey." A good-looking guy in a soccer shirt came up to Selfie. "How'd you hurt your arm?" he asked, gesturing toward her cast with an ice-cream cup.

"Come on, Selfie." I tugged her sleeve. "We've got to—"

"Volleyball accident," she said lightly. "NBD." I looked at her gratefully. "By the way, this is Becca."

"Hi, Becca." He blinked, noticing me for the first time. "I'm Harvard."

Harvard?

"That's his name," explained Selfie, reading my mind. "Harvard Thompson."

He gave me his hand to shake. Startled, I tried to slide my thumb out from under my backpack strap, but it was stuck. "Agh!" I finally pulled it loose. I wasn't used to shaking hands with teenagers. I turned to Selfie. "We have to go back and question the Fashion Clubbers," I whispered frantically. "NOW!"

When I'd finally dragged Selfie away, Roxxi and the gang had vanished. *Crud!* In this crowd, they didn't stand out; everyone looked like they'd just stepped off a sailboat.

"There's D'Nise!" I waved her down like a rescue plane, but she ignored me.

"Not HER!" Selfie hissed. "She's my bestie."

"We've got to ask *everyone*," I insisted.

Selfie sighed and summoned D'Nise with a finger wiggle. "D-Bomb!"

D'Nise strutted over, smiling. She and Selfie squealed, dapped knuckles, and reviewed each other's jewelry. When D'Nise noticed me, her smile faded. I nudged Selfie.

"Hey." Selfie smiled apologetically. "I'm looking for that, uh, *bra* I passed around the meeting. Have you . . . by any chance . . ."

"Seen it?" I jumped in.

D'Nise snorted. "You bet your butt. That thing was *monster*. I got a pic right here." She reached for her phone. *HOLY CRUD!*

I peered at the screen, horrified.

"D'Nise!" I burst out. "Can you delete that? We're trying to keep the whole thing quiet. Did you—by any chance—*take* the bra, or know who did?"

D'Nise looked astonished. "Are you accusing me?"

"NOOO!" Selfie and I cried together.

"I swear, I'll call my dad *right now*—" D'Nise fumed. Her father was a famous lawyer.

"NO!" I gasped. "Of course not! We didn't mean—"

So far, this was going great.

One down, eight to go.

• • • • •

Roxxi didn't wait for me to find her. Instead, she grabbed my arm and dragged me into the instant-photo booth.

"You're doing an 'investigation'? That's the *stupidest* thing I ever heard," she spat out. She pushed me onto the stool and stood next to it, resting a boot on the seat. "What's your problem? You think we're going to let a sixth grader harass us? At our own *club*!?"

"Um . . ." I peeked outside the curtain, looking for Selfie. She was talking to a guy in layered polo shirts.

"D'Nise is going ballistic." Roxxi's eyes blazed.

"Listen, Roxxi." I took a deep breath. "I'm doing this for Selfie. We're not accusing anyone. We just need to know if anyone has the bra or knows where it is. If Selfie doesn't find it, she's in big trouble."

"Really?" Roxxi moved closer. "What kind of trouble?"

"Well—"

"Will she be grounded from school activities?" Roxxi's eyes widened. "Dethroned from prom princess? Transferred to a Swiss boarding school?"

"Hard to predict." Was it my imagination, or did Roxxi sound . . . *excited*?

Something told me not to say more. I put my elbow down and heard a loud *CLICK*. Lights started to flash. Roxxi jumped away from the booth's wall. Five seconds later: *CLICK! CLICK! CLICK!*

CRUD! We were being photographed! I'd pushed the button by accident. "AHHHHH!" Roxxi screamed. We turned away, horrified. *CLICK! CLICK! CLICK!* Ten seconds later, there was a thrashing noise. The machine spat out the world's worst photo strip.

"Give me that!" Roxxi tried to swipe it, but I kept her away. Not that *I* wanted the photos—I just didn't want *her* to have them. I didn't trust her. We fell back into the booth, wrestling each other. "Ugh," she grunted, trying to peel my fingers off the paper. I tried to use my smallness as an advantage, curling up

into a rigid ball. Finally, I shook her loose and she tumbled backward.

YES! I slipped the photo strip into my shirt. "Those better not turn up anywhere!" Roxxi warned as she rose and brushed herself off.

"Don't worry," I said quickly.

"There you are!" Selfie slid back the curtain of the photo booth, startling both of us. Layered Polo Shirts stood next to her. Selfie looked from me to Roxxi quizzically. "Sorry, I didn't mean to interrupt! Sims and I were just—"

Roxxi stepped out of the booth, wiping off her plaid skirt. "S'all yours. We're done."

"But—" I got up and called after Roxxi. "You never told me if you saw the—"

"GOOD-BYE," she turned and shouted. "That ship has *sailed.*"

Crud! I'd won the photo-strip catfight but lost the much more important battle: squeezing info out of Roxxi.

I raced back to the photo booth but stopped outside when I heard Selfie's giggles and squeals. "Ha ha ha! *Sims!* Is that a dare?" I looked at the floor, wondering if I should barge in. It wasn't like she was a huge help with the interviews.

The room was emptying out. We had to find the other clubbers, *ASAP*. What if they'd left already?

"Vivienne!" I shrieked, like a shipwrecked sailor. "Over here!"

· · ● · ·

RINGGGG! RINGGGG!

I opened an eye. My phone was ringing. "Hullo?"

"Don't tell me I woke you up," someone said. "It's not even *nine*."

Prezbo! I must have fallen asleep after the country club disaster. My mouth was dry, and I was still in my street clothes. Something was wadded up in my hand.

The Teen Lounge—*ugh*. It all came back to me. The pool table, giant-screen TV, girls in tennis dresses, omelet station, Roxxi's blazing eyes. Trying to question Vivienne and Beckett, who were surprisingly patient and polite and totally unhelpful. Tracking down Jaden at the ice-cream-toppings bar, who "didn't see anything, I swear." Blank stares from Clementine and Lisbeth. It all added up to a big, fat *zero*.

No wonder I'd fallen asleep immediately.

I cleared my throat. "Hi."

He started talking again, but in my strange, half-awake state, I couldn't quite follow. Something about earth science homework? Now he was describing a kung fu movie. I rubbed my ear and tried to listen harder: a story about a harmonica and a meatball sandwich. I closed my eyes again.

". . . blew off the math picnic. But debate team elected a—"

The math picnic. Debate team. My old life seemed so distant now. Was it only this morning I'd had the luxury of caring about such things?

Now the only thing that mattered was getting an extra-large undergarment back to its rightful owner.

"...did *you* do this afternoon?" he finished.

"Ummm." I stalled for time. I didn't want to drop the Bra Bomb just yet. The fewer people who knew, the better. "I ended up at the Teen Lounge at the country club with Selfie. Totally weird."

"Oh." Prezbo seemed thrown off. "I thought you were at clarinet practice. What was it like?"

"Aw, you know." I tried to play it down. "Foosball, basketball hoop, stuff like that. You'd hate it. Except for the giant TV, arcade games, and free food."

"WHAT?" His voice went up. "Slow down! What kind of food?"

"Just, you know, omelets, sushi, mini tacos, ice cream ..." I mumbled.

"Mini tacos?" He sounded pained.

"Yeah, but—" I'd forgotten what a big eater he was. "The people were snobs."

"Well, *duh*," he said. "What were you doing there?"

Reasonable question. Something under my shirt itched horribly. I reached into it and felt a paper edge. The photo strip of me and Roxxi! "Remember that thing I picked up for Selfie from the principal? I was with her, and she wanted to stop at the club."

"Oh. Right." Finally, he was losing interest. "Reason I called was, I'm not doing my video segment tomorrow, so—"

"Really? Why not?" I asked. As long as I could remember, Prezbo spent Thursday lunch at the school recording studio, taping video game reviews for *Action News*. He loved being a video game critic.

"Robson called it off." I could feel Prezbo's grimace. He always complained about Rob Robson, the self-important eighth-grade anchor of *Action News*, who treated the closed-circuit TV show like it was *60 Minutes*.

"Supposedly, he's got an exclusive scoop on some huge"—Prezbo put on a fake news announcer's voice— "top secret, mind-boggling, senses-shattering, eye-popping, outrageous, you've-got-to-see-it-to-believe-it prank." Prezbo snorted. "That's what he says, anyway."

My heart stopped.

Top secret? Mind-boggling?

"What kind of prank?" I swallowed.

Chapter 7

*D*on't jump to conclusions! My heart pounded like crazy as I waited for Selfie outside school. This "mind-boggling" prank didn't have to involve the principal's underwear. The timing was pure coincidence. Chances were, it had nothing—*nothing!*—to do with us.

But every instinct told me otherwise.

I looked at my watch. We *had* to find the bra; failure was *not* an option. Any moment, Dr. Valentine would discover the Great Shopping Bag Mix-up. What would happen if we had to say, "We lost it"?

Finally, the long black car pulled up. A high-heeled bootie emerged, followed by artfully shredded denim and an acre of black-silk trench coat. With big sun-glasses, jumbo coffee cup, and messy updo, her look was classic rock-star-at-the-airport.

"Thank God you're here!" I ran up to Selfie, star-tling her. As she sipped coffee, I told her about our only lead: Rob Robson, the school news anchor, was about to broadcast an outrageous prank, which might or might not involve a certain plus-size personal item. We had to rush to the *Action News* office to find out.

"Shhhhh." She held a finger to her lips. "No talk-ing yet. Late night. Barely awake."

"Oh—" I stopped abruptly. I had never seen Early Morning Selfie. When she took off her sunglasses, her eyes looked puffy and sleep-deprived. Maybe the whole mess with the principal had taken its toll on her, too. "What happened?"

Selfie rubbed her temples. "Sims and I snuck out to his dad's yacht. FYI? Never water-ski at midnight."

"*You* water-skied—" My voice rose. "In an ARM CAST?"

"No loud noises. I only got four hours' sleep."

As the halls filled up with students, we sprinted toward the *Action News* office. I tried to explain, once again, the seriousness of our situation. How *desperately* we needed to get the bra back.

"Too bright!" Selfie protested when we hit the harsh lights of the Media Wing. But we were out of luck—the office was closed.

"Crud." I rubbed my forehead. I didn't have a plan B. *Think*, I told myself. *Think! You need intel on this prank*. Who knew about pranks?

Suddenly, I knew exactly where to go.

· · ● · ·

"Forged hall pass? Locker break-in? Stink bomb?"

Ajax Webber didn't look up from his phone. He rattled off the list in a bored mono- tone, sitting on a trash can under the stairwell. Selfie and I stood next to him awkwardly.

"Fire alarm? Bath- room flood? Fake per- mission slip?" He kept going.

I turned to Ajax. "Actually—"

"Need someone iced?" His voice got lower.

Seriously? "No! We—"

Ajax was the school's most high-profile bully. He and his friends, Scab Czarek and B.B. "Big Bite" Blanchard, were known for fights, intimidation, and control of the East Annex stairwell. Together they formed the Piranhas, the school's only gang. It was said that, like an international bank, they had branches in other locations.

They were also known for pulling pranks.

Filling a teacher's car with packing peanuts. Liberating lab rats. Redecorating the school dance.

After a pair of teachers passed, we squeezed in closer under the stairwell, the center of illicit activity at JGMS. Anything could be bought or arranged here, supposedly.

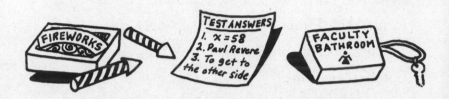

"Spit it out already." Ajax sounded irritated. "I'm busy." His phone screen said, AN UNUSUAL FRIENDSHIP BETWEEN A BEAR AND A DACHSHUND. B.B. circled like a buzzard, while Scab seemed to be trying to set something on fire.

"Um . . ." Maybe this wasn't such a good idea. "We heard about the big prank. And we just want to know—"

His eyes looked blank. "What prank?"

Of course, he had to deny it. "Don't worry," I assured him. "We just need to know if—"

"Know what?" Ajax looked genuinely stumped. "We haven't done jack since the dead ferret."

Should I tell him? "There's supposed to be a huge prank today, and Rob Robson's filming it."

"ROBSON?" Ajax jumped up.

"He's not *doing* the prank," Selfie explained patiently as she shook her hair loose. "He's broadcasting it. Supposedly it's some top secret, maj freaky event, and Rob's catching it on film. . . ."

"WHAT?" Ajax roared. "He never filmed *my* pranks!"

Awkward. "I'm sure it's nowhere near as good as the Homeroom Saran Wrap or Butt Xerox Wallpaper," I said, naming his greatest hits.

Ajax glared at Scab and B.B. "Well, don't stand there with your mouths open. Why are we the last to know? What do you guys do all day? HOMEWORK!?"

Scab and B.B. looked at the floor.

"Let's go," I whispered to Selfie.

"NO!" Ajax barked. "Not till we get all the info. Where's this prank? Who's doing it?"

"We hoped *you* could tell *us*!" I said.

"Hunh." Ajax stroked his chin. He stomped around, muttering swear words under his breath. After a few minutes, he turned to us. "Okay, okay. Let's say I *did* get you the goods. What's in it for me?"

His eyes had a definite gleam.

"Well!" I said, getting into bargain mode. I wasn't student council secretary for nothing. "Lots of things! Extra cafeteria desserts? Featured yearbook pic? School hoodie?"

"Those suck." Ajax spit on the ground.

"Oh. *Oh.*" I looked at Selfie, desperate for ideas. "Jazz-band tee? Premium seats for Spring Sing? School stationery?" *Crud.*

Selfie jumped in. "Fashion Passion gift card? Vintage jeans? Tix to the Golf and Tennis Gala?"

"Get lost." Ajax started shoving things into his backpack.

"Book tote?" I shouted. "School-logo water bottle?"

He started down the hall.

"Ajax!" Selfie bolted after him. "WAIIIIIITTTTT!"

Surprised, I watched her leap after him like a gazelle and grab his jacket.

"I've got it," she said to him, out of breath. "How'd you like to be number one on the Hottie List in the girls' bathroom?"

"Done," he said.

After Ajax and his friends bolted, I turned to Selfie, impressed. "Whoa!" I said. "That was brilliant. I didn't even know there *was* a Hottie List!"

Selfie gave me an *oh-you're-so-naive* smile while she applied lipstick. "There's not," she said. "You're going to make one."

"Me?" I felt my stomach clench.

"Yeah." She reached into her massive purse and handed me a pen topped by a fluffy hot-pink feather. It wasn't a pen for writing a book report or a paper on Thomas Jefferson. It was a pen you used to write an entry in a slam book or a fan letter to a boy band.

"Okay." I took it uneasily. Right now we had bigger things to worry about. Heading toward us was Selfie's posse—D'Nise, Chaz, Roxxi, Vivienne, Margaux. Last night, we'd given them the third degree about the missing—*ahem*—item. Now they were charging toward us like a noisy army.

"You ever find that monster bra?"

"What a freak show."

"Ovah-the-shouldah-bouldah-holdah!"

"Told you I didn't have it!"

"SHHHHHHHH!" I was frantic. "Voices down—*please*! This is SUPER, *mega*-top secret—"

They got even louder.

"We must . . . we must . . . we must increase our BUST." Chaz swung back his elbows, doing pretend exercises, and everyone laughed.

I looked at Selfie helplessly, but she just shrugged, as if to say, *What can you do?* Asking this group to shut up was like asking fish not to swim. Even though we'd sworn and double-sworn the Fashion Clubbers to secrecy about the bra, I should have known they'd be buzzing about it the second they hit the halls.

How long before the rest of the school caught on?

"We are so dead," I whispered to Selfie, feeling my head throb. "Look at all these people. . . ." I spread my arms to the larger sea of students flooding the halls. "Any one of them could've overheard those guys blabbing about it!"

"Not him." Selfie pointed to a lone kid slicing through the crowded hall, eyes on his gaming device, ears plugged into headphones. I recognized Felix Needleman, a nerdy sixth grader in a thick sweater and too-short corduroys. He carried a superhero tote bag, probably a giveaway from Comic-Con. Boy, was he out of it.

"If he didn't, he's the only one." I snort-laughed. Okay, so maybe one oddball, unibrowed, gaming freak didn't mix with the gossip crowd. That still left everyone else.

WHOMP! Somebody grabbed Selfie and me and pushed us into a doorway, kidnapper-style. We both yelped. When we opened our eyes, Ajax stood in front of us, panting.

"Mission accomplished." He wiped sweat off his forehead.

"Is that how you say hi?" I asked, annoyed.

"Do you want info or not?" he asked.

"Yeah." I steeled myself.

"At twelve thirty," he said, "the principal's bra's going up the flagpole."

Chapter 8

*T*HUMP! *THUMP! THUMP!*

"Rob! We know you're there!"

Selfie and I pounded on the door of the *Action News* office, trying to get Rob Robson to come out. I'd met him before when I came with Prezbo to record video game reviews. Everyone knew Rob as the school-news anchor. He was also a sleazebag who'd do anything for ratings.

The door opened, and a short guy with glasses stuck his head out. "Rob's busy," he said, shutting it again.

THUMP! THUMP! THUMP!

"Open up!" I shouted. "Or we'll file a report with the . . . the . . . Middle School Broadcast Journalists' Board of Ethics!"

The door opened a crack.

Selfie and I burst into the "newsroom"—really just a couple of desks and a copy machine. *CBS Evening News,* it wasn't. In past years, stories would include an interview with the school nurse about flu season or a preview of decorations for the Glow-in-the-Dark Dance.

But Rob was trying to change all that. The show's motto was "Fast-breaking School News—As It Happens!" He was the first on the scene at a skateboard accident or girls' locker-room fight. Some said his stories went too far.

Rob was with two other reporters. "What do you want?" His eyes were glued to a TV camera, which he was showing to the short guy with glasses and a skinny seventh grader. The extreme mess suggested the kind of round-the-clock work sessions associated with covering presidential elections or terrorist events. The short guy nudged him and pointed at us.

Rob saw Selfie and leaped up. "Hey! Hey, hey." He smoothed down his T-shirt and brushed off his jeans. Being around Selfie made people do that. Then he started flinging away fast-food cartons to clear a seat.

"We don't have time to sit," I jumped in. "We heard about this prank you're filming, and we want it stopped. *Immediately.*"

They all gasped.

"Whoa, whoa, *whoa.*" Rob cupped his ear. "WHAT?"

He looked so astonished I wondered if we'd gotten it wrong.

"The prank." I suddenly felt shy, accusing a very high-profile eighth grader. "Is . . . is it true?"

"*Is* it?" From Selfie, it sounded flirtatious.

Rob folded his arms defiantly, but his eyes kept sliding toward Selfie. "How in the world . . . ? That's TOP SECRET. I don't discuss ongoing stories."

AHA! So it *was* true! He'd all but admitted it! I felt a little thrill of victory, before a wave of nausea hit me.

"Who *are* you, anyway?" asked one of the other guys.

"Becca Birnbaum." I stood up straighter. "I was here before with Prezbo. Plus I'm secretary of the student council," I added, hoping to sound important.

Giggles broke out. "Why should we listen to you?" one guy asked.

"Cuz you should." Selfie lifted her head like a queen. "She knows things! About laws and stuff."

"And how are you two, uh . . ." Rob looked quizzically from me to Selfie. "Connected?"

"It doesn't matter," I said. "What matters is, you have to shut this thing down. Or we can have you . . ." Their mocking faces made me feel desperate. *"Arrested."*

"HA HA HA!" The guys exploded with laughter, poking one another. "On what grounds?"

"On grounds of . . ." *What did they say on cop shows?* "Accomplice to a crime. Aiding—and abetting. Abetting and aiding. The school authorities would be *very* interested." It never hurt to throw in "school authorities."

The three of them grew a shade paler. "Listen, Beckett—" Rob walked over and got up in my face.

"Becca."

"Becca, I'm not doing anything wrong!" His eyes locked with mine. "The prank is *news*. Covering news is my *job*."

This was maddening. "But, Rob, you're *creating* news! You don't have to help this JERK by giving him publicity!"

He pressed even closer to me, narrowing his eyes as if deeply hurt. "Becky, do you think . . . you think I do this for *myself*?"

Oh, *brother*. "It's Becca."

"I do it for my AUDIENCE!" he exploded. His eyes stole another glance at Selfie, who was rubbing lotion on her elbows. "The average joe who tunes in after a boring day of prime numbers and Fun With Phonics. Does he want to hear about the Woodshop Awards? Or the Ice Cream Social?"

"I'm not—" I started.

"NO FREAKIN' WAY!" He puffed out his chest, eyes straying toward Selfie again. Now she was reading a magazine. "He—or, you know, she—wants fights. Explosions. Accidents. Public barfings. *Real life*."

"Rob—"

"As a famous war correspondent said . . . ," he started. The other two guys slumped in their chairs, settling in for a long speech. Rob looked hopefully at Selfie, his voice swelling as he ranted on about journalism and embeds and the guts to tell the real story.

"STOPPPP!" I covered my ears. "I can't take it!"

Everyone looked at me.

"Rob, we're *begging* you." My voice softened. "Think of what this'll actually look like: that flagpole on every school TV screen! Embarrassing the principal would be . . . *horrible*. She's—she's tough, but she's okay. You don't want to do that; I know you don't."

Rob's eyes narrowed. "And why do you care?"

I bit my lip. Even if I hadn't had a hand in this disaster, humiliating the principal was wrong. It was too mean. Valentine was no fan of mine, but she didn't deserve this—no one did. "Because it's the right thing to do," I said quietly.

"Meeting's over, Birnbaum," he said grimly. *"Back off."*

Now I was beyond desperate. "This is just a ratings grab," I shouted. "So they don't turn this room into a yoga studio!"

"Don't let the door hit you on your way out." He went back to his video camera.

I felt a surge of panic. We had to pry *something* out of Rob—a name, a lead, a clue. We couldn't just go back out there and wait for catastrophe. "At least say who's doing the prank," I pleaded. "Then we'll get lost, I promise!"

Rob's head snapped up.

"Reveal a source?" His voice rose in outrage.

"Never. NEVER! Let 'em throw me in jail. But I won't compromise my journalistic integrity."

"Gimme a break!" I burst out. He'd reached new heights—or depths—of bogusness.

"It's called reporter's privilege. Look it up," he snarled.

"We'll let the principal decide!" I shot back.

The mood in the room turned deadly serious, and my own words chilled me. Was I really willing to go to the principal? I remembered how angry she was at Selfie and how unfriendly she'd been to me. I really, really didn't want to involve her—but if I had to, I would.

"You're not *going* to tell the principal," Robson said slowly. "Or any other faculty member. 'Cause if I hear you breathed a *word* . . ." He smiled. "Your little buddy Prezbo just recorded his last video game review."

What? He wouldn't *dare*! Prezbo loved that job more than anything. He always wore a fresh band tee every

Thursday and his baddest, most beat-up sneakers. He got a huge, crooked smile on his face when he talked about it. Robson wouldn't be that cruel . . . *would he?*

Grrrrrr.

I couldn't do that to Prezbo. "Let's go, Selfie, this is—"

But Selfie was in the middle of a selfie. She was squinting at the phone and trying different angles. "Can you hold my stuff for a minute?" I took her magazine, lotion bottle, and shopping bag.

"Selfie, *please!*" I shoved her stuff into my backpack. It was hard to make an angry exit with her snapping away.

She took one more shot and then slipped the phone into her pocket. She gave Rob a look of smoldering disgust, muttering something in French that ended in *stupide*.

"This is your last chance to do the right thing!" I shouted.

He pushed us out the door.

· · ● · ·

"Becca? Is that YOU?" Rosa looked puzzled to see me writing on the wall in the girls' bathroom.

Startled, I yanked my hands from the pale pink surface. *NOOOO!* My heart sank. I'd deliberately waited until the bathroom was empty. Of all people to walk in, why did it have to be *Rosa*?

"What are you doing?" she asked.

"Nothing." I leaned on the wall, trying to hide the markings. But she edged me aside to see it.

"You're writing a ... HOTTIE LIST?" She stared in horror.

My stomach lurched. "Yeah, but—"

"Number one, Ajax Webber. Number two, Jonah Belasco. Number three—" Rosa read out loud. "You've got to be kidding." The outrage in her eyes said hottie lists were not only repellent but also a betrayal of our principles.

My head was throbbing. "Rosa, I swear! It—this doesn't have anything to do with me! It's payback for . . . ugh, it's a long story—" How could I tell it in a couple of sentences?

"We don't do stuff like this." Her eyes were still fixed on me. "*We make fun of* people who do stuff like this."

"Just listen!" I begged, trying to cover Selfie's ridiculous pink feather pen with my fist.

"Yesterday," Rosa continued, "you were a normal, if reasonably twisted, human being, who would be appalled at any number of things: hottie lists, selfie sticks, eye makeup, golf cart theft, people who wear three-inch heels to school, Fashion Club, pink feather pens—"

"I still am!" I pleaded. "C'mon, give me some credit—"

"So I have to conclude the evil influence here is one long-legged, rich, blond party girl," Rosa interrupted.

"No! NO! It's not 'cause of her! I mean, *technically*, maybe, but—"

Rosa snorted.

Desperate, I grabbed Rosa's shoulders and tried again. "Five minutes, Rosa, give me FIVE MINUTES!" I lowered my voice. "It all started yesterday, when—"

The bathroom door banged open. A few sixth graders streamed in and then a group of older girls.

I tried to move away from the list, but people saw the words on the wall and swarmed around to read it. Suddenly, there was a big crowd, and Rosa and I were trapped.

"Ajax, number one? That's a joke, right?"

"EW!"

"Why isn't Rakim on here?"

"Brad Copeland's *ninth*?"

Run, I told myself, but Rosa and I were squashed against the wall. People jumped up, clawing and shoving to get a better look.

"MOVE!" shouted a voice I knew but couldn't quite place. "THIS LIST IS ILLEGAL! Cross it out NOW!"

I looked up, expecting to see a teacher, but it was Roxxi, pointing a finger above the crowd. *CRUD!* I wasn't up for another tangle with her. She elbowed her way to the front and got in my face.

"Haven't you caused enough trouble for one week?" Her voice was dripping with fury. "You barge into the country club, then—"

Rosa's eyes widened at the words *country club*.

"You accuse everyone of taking that stupid bra." Roxxi narrowed her eyes. So much for keeping it a secret. "Why is it so important to you, anyway?"

Bra!?? Rosa mouthed.

"And now you write a school HOTTIE LIST!?" Roxxi's voice rose even higher. She was as outraged as Rosa but for totally different reasons. "Where do you get the *nerve*? If anyone gets to, it should be a responsible eighth grader who has the experience and position to—"

"BOOOOOO!" someone hissed.

Roxxi blinked.

A girl turned to Roxxi. "So what you're saying is," she said, "the 'cool' clique should take it over, like they take over EVERYTHING ELSE at this school?"

"They suck!"

"Tell it, girl!"

"BOOOOO!"

Roxxi's face turned pink. People were whistling, laughing, and pumping their fists.

I looked at Rosa, to see if she was enjoying this spontaneous Anti-Clique Bathroom Rebellion, but she refused to meet my eyes.

"Come on, Roxxi." Vivienne Ling put an arm around her. "Ignore 'em."

"No!" Roxxi stamped her foot. "Cross out the list! NOW!"

A blond head suddenly appeared above the crowd, like a skyscraper catching the light. Her blue eyes were level with Roxxi's.

"The list stays," Selfie said with quiet authority. A hush came over the bathroom. "Come on, Becca; we've got work to do."

"Uh-huh, oh *yeah,* uh-huh, oh *yeah—*" Some girls did a cheer.

Roxxi's eyes flashed with anger, but she saw she was outnumbered. *You've won this one,* her face seemed to say, *but the war ain't over.*

As Selfie beckoned me with a manicured finger, Rosa looked at me with a disgust reserved for litterers, high-fiving jocks, and people who dress up for School Colors Day. I wanted to fly to her side and beg forgiveness. How could I explain the roller-coaster ride of the past twenty-four hours? Having weirdness with Rosa made me sick to my stomach.

But seeing Selfie with the principal's Sandstrom's bag in her hand, I knew what I had to do.

I nodded to Selfie. "Let's go."

The crowd refused to scatter. "You're not going to fight?" A girl looked from Roxxi to Selfie, disappointed.

"No. But if you really want excitement . . ." Roxxi's eyes swept the crowd. "GO TO THE FLAGPOLE TODAY AT TWELVE THIRTY!"

We gasped.

"See, Selfie?" Roxxi smiled sweetly. "There are some things even *you* can't stop."

Chapter 9

"*T*HERE YOU ARE!"

Walking down the hall during passing period, we turned to see who was shouting at us. Mr. Maslon, the principal's secretary, raced toward us with something under his arm. We watched in shock as he made a beeline for Selfie, who was carrying Dr. Valentine's shopping bag.

"I'll take that!" Maslon lunged at Selfie, snatching the bag. It happened so fast she didn't have time to react. "And this belongs to *you*," he said, handing her a different Sandstrom's bag.

"Oh!" Selfie clutched the bag, blinking.

We stared at him, astonished.

"Just in time!" He panted. "Principal's back at twelve forty-five."

Fifteen minutes after Robson's broadcast.

"Um—" Words wouldn't come out.

"Thank God I found you," Maslon said. "Before Dr. Valentine discovered the mix-up. Because if *something happened to this bag*? Let's just say: Detention wouldn't cover it. Suspension wouldn't cover it. Hard to say what would."

Selfie and I gulped.

"Have you"—Maslon dropped to a whisper— *"looked inside?"*

Now we were trapped. Point-blank questions were dangerous. I wanted to ... reassure him somehow, but I didn't want to lie.

"Just long enough to realize it wasn't ours," I said.

Maslon pulled us aside. He took a deep breath. "Then you understand how, uh—*sensitive*—the situation is."

"Yes," I croaked out.

Maslon gripped my shoulder, his eyes piercing mine. "You can never, EVER breathe a word of this."

We shook our heads furiously.

"To anyone."

We nodded, sinking further into the floor.

"Good!" His voice lifted as he backed away. "It's nice to know *some* students can be trusted. Now I can drop this on the principal's desk and never look at it again. What a relief!"

Selfie and I stood there, frozen. Neither of us had the nerve to tell him the bra wasn't in there.

· · ● · ·

We were frantic. Going to class was out of the question; we *had* to locate the bra. Unfortunately, we had no idea where to look. My mind went wild, imagining it in different places around school.

We kept asking Fashion Club people if they'd seen it. "I heard the science lab skeleton's wearing that monster bra," said D'Nise. "Rocking it, too."

That was the problem. Everyone had "heard" something, but no one would admit to having it. "Talk to D'Nise," someone would say. "She saw it." When we found D'Nise, she'd say, "I think KeShawn has it." KeShawn would shrug. "Ask Vanessa." Vanessa said, "Brooklyn knows." "How do I know?" Brooklyn asked. "Talk to D'Nise."

It was only a matter of time before the Incredible Bra Story seeped out into the general population.

I looked at my watch—11:00.

Showtime is in an hour and a half.

We'd hit rock bottom. Slumped on benches in the girls' locker room, Selfie and I stared at the wall. We didn't have anywhere else to go. Our weird, we're-in-it-together adventure now seemed doomed and pathetic.

Was this really me, hiding in the girls' locker room after cutting class? Before today, I'd never so much as written "you suck" in a textbook. But in the past two hours, I'd consulted a bully, defaced school property, misled an adult, let down my best friend, and skipped out on homeroom, history, and earth science. And the day wasn't over yet.

Worst of all, though, was the feeling I'd failed Selfie. I'd blown the chance to show her I had something to offer. Because despite what I'd been through because of her, I still wanted her to like me. I enjoyed her different take on the world, her made-up words, and easy kindness. I liked how she could be goofy one minute and then silence an entire cafeteria with the arch of an eyebrow. And for someone rich enough to have a beauty salon in her house, she was surprisingly appreciative. There was nothing sweeter than her breathless thanks, followed by "Becca! You're *amaze*."

But now that was all over. After today's nuclear-level disaster, friendship was out of the question. I'd just be lucky if she didn't hate me.

A door banged open, shattering my trance. A couple of eighth-grade girls stomped through the locker room. "...going to Robson's show?" one of them asked.

"Cassidy's saving me a seat," said the second one.

"Supposed to be juicy."

The second one snorted. "After all the hype? It *better* be."

Selfie and I looked at each other in horror.

CRUD!

Word was getting around fast. Even if most kids at school didn't yet know about the missing bra—or didn't believe it—Rob had them psyched for a Major Scandal. People smelled blood.

And Roxxi was right: There wasn't a thing we could do to stop it.

"Diet croissant?" Selfie took a flaky pastry out of her purse.

"No, thanks." I shook my head.

"Should we dig up more Fashion Clubbers?" Selfie started to get up. "Ask if they've seen—"

"No." I couldn't hide my gloom.

"Just . . . 'no'?" Selfie looked alarmed.

I kicked the wall.

"No," I said bluntly. "How're we going to find the you-know-what, sneak it back to the principal's office, get it into that shopping bag—"

"Well, we could—" Selfie started.

". . . *in little over an HOUR?*" My voice drowned her out. "It's not going to happen!"

Silence.

My outburst left us both rattled. We sank even lower on the bench. After a few minutes, I felt her body shaking. Drops of moisture dotted her silk scarf. Turning to look at her face, I saw tears in her eyes.

"I'm scared, Becca." Selfie's voice was thick. "I get in trouble a lot, but this feels different."

Seeing her crumple made something twist inside of me. Those sad, wet eyes! I tried to give her a side-hug, but my arm got stuck behind her and the wall. "Ow," I said, pulling it out. We were both miserable.

"I could legit get kicked out of Garfield." Now Selfie was out-and-out crying. But I was too flattened to manage more than a few awkward knee pats.

"It'll be okay," I lied.

"You don't get it," she spat out between sobs. "School's not the only place I'm messing up. Even *before* this happened, my parents were threatening to send me away—"

A jolt of alarm went through me. "Away!"

Selfie wiped her eyes. "To Chalet-Do-Nothing."

"What?"

"Chalet Du Notting. A school in Switzerland that's a joke. Where parents dump their problem kids. You know: Bring your own horse, mountain climb for gym. Live in a castle and ski to class."

Whoa.

"Sounds awful," I joked, forgetting our troubles for a minute. Selfie's not wanting to go to a rich-kid playground was interesting. Was she more into school than she let on?

"It's *heinous.*" Selfie cried harder. "Everyone there is a prince or count. They treat Americans like dog barf. Forget being popular, unless you own a Caribbean island or your dad was in the Beatles."

I just sat there with my mouth open. *Wow.* There was a place that made even *Selfie* feel small?

"You know, Selfie?" I hesitated. "That's how most of us feel every day. Like the game's rigged. 'Cause we don't have great hair, or soccer trophies, or live on Lake Drive. We're not invited to that hilarious can-you-top-this-ugly-sweater party at Chaz Green's. At school we're about as important as a substitute gym teacher."

Selfie stopped crying and stared.

"Just sayin'." *Why had I blurted that out?*

Wiping her eyes, she seemed to sink into an even deeper gloom.

"I wouldn't want to go to that Swiss school, either," I said in solidarity. "I'm scared, too. Seriously."

We were quiet again. Selfie took out her phone, clutching it like a lost BFF. Her fingers darted across the screen. Something on it was extremely absorbing. After a few more taps, she snorted. "Pwuh!"

I felt left out. "What are you doing?"

"Looking at pics." Selfie's eyes stayed on the screen.

"Oh."

She tapped the screen a few more times, releasing a half giggle, harrumph, "ugh," and "What a *freak*." Geez, how many photos did the girl take?

Just sitting there felt stupid. "Could I . . . ?"

She showed me the phone while she continued to scroll through photos.

"Wait!" I pointed to the screen. "Go back to that one."

She went back to a pic of the newsroom.

"Make it bigger!" My breathing got quicker.

Selfie obeyed.

"Becca, what is it?"

I jumped up, excited. There wasn't time to talk.

"Grab your purse," I said. "I think I know who's got the bra."

Chapter 10

I stood at the door of Prezbo's classroom, waving wildly at him through the window. Finally, I caught his attention. *I need to talk to you*, I mouthed. He gave a shrug that said, *What do you want me to do? I'm in class.*

His teacher, Mr. De Santo, saw me and opened the door. "Can I help you, Becca?"

"I need to talk to Prezbo." I gulped.

"What's this about?" His voice was clipped.

"Can you tell him..." My mind raced. *What sounded urgent enough?* "His, uh, locker is on fire."

Mr. De Santo lowered his voice. "What?"

"His locker is on fire." I coughed. *Add this to my criminal list of "firsts,"* I thought. I'd never lied to a teacher and dragged someone out of class before.

De Santo went back into class and whispered to Prezbo, and he bolted over to me.

"There's a fire?" He came to the classroom door out of breath, and I closed it behind us.

"Are there shooting flames? Explosions? Noxious gases? Hazmat suits?" His face lit up.

"What? No! Prez, I lied. There's no fire."

"WHAT?" His eyes widened.

"Forget it. Your locker's not on fire." I waved my hand. "I had to get you out here somehow. Sorry."

Prezbo's mouth dropped open. "I can't believe you made that up." He sounded half-annoyed, half-impressed.

There wasn't time to explain.

"I need intel—ASAP. What do you know about Felix Needleman?"

Prezbo's eyebrows shot up. "You dragged me out here to ask about *Felix Needleman*?"

I nodded apologetically.

"I'll tell you why later—promise!" My eyes begged. "Right now I need everything you've got: schedule, likes and dislikes, lunch table, extracurris, aliases, obsessions, criminal record, pet peeves, fave pizza toppings, dream date, boxers or briefs, innie or outie, whatever."

Prezbo stared.

"What am I, *Teen Crush Magazine*?" He looked annoyed. "How do I know?"

"Prez." I lowered my voice. "Felix is in sixth grade. He's computer-y. He wears weird hats. I know you've got the scoop on him. I'm desperate!"

"Okay, okay." Prezbo scowled, folding his arms.

"Let's go to the East Stairwell. Selfie's waiting," I said.

"Selfie! *The* Selfie?" He frowned. After scanning his shirt for food stains, he pulled up his belt and gave his underarm a sniff.

As we walked there, Prezbo said, "By the way, what did you say to Rosa? She thinks you've turned into some shallow, fashion-obsessed airhead."

"What? That's crazy." I snorted, just as Selfie's stuff tumbled out of my backpack. Prezbo picked up one of her magazines.

"I-it's not mine . . . ," I stammered.

"Right." Prezbo stooped to collect the rest of the junk.

When we swung open the door to the stairwell, Selfie was sitting on the stairs holding her phone at different angles near her foot. As I got closer, I realized she was photographing one of her high-heeled boots. Prezbo looked puzzled. "Oh, hi." She glanced up at us. "I'm taking a shoefie."

"This is Prezbo," I announced as I sat next to her. "He's going to brief us on Felix."

"Hi." Selfie flashed a smile.

"Greetings." Prezbo swallowed. "You probably don't recognize me, but our lockers are kitty-corner. Actually, that's only semi-accurate. It's not a true diagonal."

Selfie blinked. Clearly, she'd never seen him before. To popular eighth graders, sixth graders were
invisible.

"Or you might know me from *Action News*," Prezbo
babbled on. "I review video games. Top sellers, but also
more obscure ones. I try to include a range."

"Oh. Okay. Wow." Selfie nodded. "You do look
kind of familiar. Do you play golf?"

"*Golf?*" Prezbo looked offended. "No. *No!* Do you
ever go to jazz band concerts? Sometimes I play tri-
angle. And I ran lights at the Environmental Fair. On
weekends—"

"Let's get down to business," I interrupted, before
Prezbo gave his whole schedule. Why on earth was
he talking a mile a minute about things she had no
interest in? It had to be The Selfie Effect. She turned
guys into mutes, idiots, or show-offs.

I pulled his pants leg to nudge him.

"Felix. Right." He cleared his throat. "Um . . . he's kind of a nerd's nerd. He makes *me* look like a chest-bumping football jock. Reads manga in Japanese. Carries eight-sided role-playing dice in his wallet. On weekends, you can find him at Star Wars Trivia Night, magic lessons, or toy band practice. His backpack is the size of a mini-fridge and has a monk's robe and bottle of fake blood. Other questions?"

"Good." I nodded. "More."

"Dream date?" Prezbo stroked his chin. "Take-out roast pig from Medieval Castle and a documentary on medical blunders."

"Ooh." Selfie winced.

"Let's see, what else does he like . . ." Prezbo's voice deepened as he shot a glance at Selfie. He was enjoying the attention. "Flame wars. Hacking into websites. Being first to reveal top secret movie plotlines. Internet poker. Pulling pranks. YouTube videos with turtles in them. Weird-flavored jelly beans—"

PRANKS?

My breath stopped.

"Did you say . . . pranks?"

"Yeah." Prezbo shrugged. "He's into pranks. A couple of weeks ago, he tried to sell the school on Craigslist."

"Keep going." My heart was beating wildly.

"He's small-time but trying to make a name for himself. Wants to get in the big leagues, with eighth graders like Ajax Webber. But that's a high bar. You'd have to do something really *epic*."

"Epic," I repeated, dazed.

"You know—sneak a horse into gym. Have a hundred pizzas delivered to the principal. Stuff like that. Ajax has been number one at pranks as long as I can remember." Prezbo's voice held a respect he reserved for the founder of Apple, cult film directors, and certain Marvel Comics inkers.

"Prezbo." I jumped up and squeezed his arm. "This is great. Just tell us where to find him, and you can go back to class."

He started protesting. "But I haven't told you about his fantasy hockey club. . . ."

"Yikes!" I looked at my watch. "We've got to go."

"Oh, no, you don't." Prezbo blocked the door. "You can't pull me out of class like it's DEFCON four and not tell me what this is about!"

I felt ashamed. I'd treated him badly—keeping

secrets, making emergency demands, and then trying to cut him loose. I couldn't put him off any longer. Prezbo was smart, blunt, and honorable. He tells you when you've messed up. I trusted his judgment and usually took his advice.

The trouble was, I was scared to hear it.

"Okay." I swallowed. "It all started when . . ."

· · ● · ·

"Go to the principal," Prezbo said. "Immediately."

Just what I was afraid of.

We had moved to the boiler room, where I'd spilled the whole tragic story. Prezbo and I were sitting on a giant pipe, while Selfie leaned against a water tank to protect her clothes. "Eew!" She jumped back. "There's a bug in here the size of a Lexus."

Prezbo and I barely heard her. We were in serious debate mode.

"You've got to tell Valentine what Robson's about to do!" Prezbo's voice was urgent. "It's your only option."

It *wasn't* an option—but I couldn't tell Prezbo why.

Rob Robson's warning rang in my ears. *'Cause if I hear you breathed a word...your little buddy Prezbo just recorded his last video game review.* After listening to Prezbo proudly tell Selfie about his job, I couldn't do that to him. And I didn't want to reveal Robson's threat and make him feel bad.

"Otherwise, you're going to have a total freakin' disaster on your hands," he said.

"Well, we can't go to the principal," I said.

"No way." Selfie moved to the pipe. "She totally has it in for me! Someday I want back all the stuff she's confiscated. Especially the leg waxer."

Prezbo blinked at her.

"I'm just worried. . . ." He frowned. "What if it comes out later you had a chance to stop it and didn't?"

My hands suddenly felt cold. "I'd rather stop it some other way."

Prezbo sighed heavily and kicked the concrete floor. "I wish you had told me earlier."

"I know." Looking back, I knew it had been stupid not to. His brain would have come in handy. "But it was so, SO top secret. We didn't want people to—"

"I'm not 'people.'" Prezbo sounded insulted.

"No, you're not." I shook my head sincerely. He was Prezbo—the best un-boyfriend a girl could have.

"Why do you think it's Felix?" he asked.

"Because of this." Selfie handed over her phone with the photo on it. I enlarged it.

"See?" I pointed to the baseball hat on the table. "There's his hat in the newsroom. He must have come to the office right before us! Plus you said he's dying to pull a major prank. It just makes sense."

Prezbo stroked his chin. "True, this would be Needleman's chance to make a big splash. How would he have gotten the bra, though? You said it disappeared at Fashion Club."

Selfie nodded. "Right after Prom Hair Dos and Don'ts."

"Who knows?" I shrugged.

"Maybe you could bribe him not to do it. Let's see, what could you offer . . . tickets to a jousting tournament? Skybox at Comic-Con? Double-Mylar-bagged first issue of Cyclopterous?" Prezbo sighed again. "Are you *sure* you don't want to go to the principal?"

Selfie and I nodded.

"Okay." He shrugged. "It's your funeral."

"Just tell us where to find Needleman," I said. "We'll see if it's really him and try to talk him out of it."

Prezbo looked at his watch. "He's in the Media Lab. At the far end of the room, four guys will be at the conference table with their laptops, supposedly working on a group project. They're actually playing *ScepterQuest*. Drag Felix away to talk in private."

"How do I do that?" I asked.

Prezbo smiled. "Tell him his locker's on fire."

Standing at the door of the Media Lab, Selfie and I studied Felix through the window. Just as Prezbo had predicted, he and three other tech geeks sat at a table, looking suspiciously absorbed in schoolwork. The teacher, Mrs. Kavanaugh, was on the opposite end of the room, hunched over a computer with other students.

I nudged Selfie. "Let's do this."

CRAAACK. I opened the door and we slipped in. Hardly anyone seemed to notice as we skirted the Media Lab. Students were clustered at tables, working on group projects. A closer look revealed gossiping, hair braiding, and online shopping. We hid behind a computer terminal where we could eavesdrop on Felix and his friends.

"I'll give you two hundred groth for the land between the Elf Kingdom and Oorwyn Castle."

"Get lost. That land was conquered in the Formic Wars."

"In that case, I'll slay the dragon."

"Goat dung! I banish you to a pit of cobras. Roll to see how miserably you die."

Selfie and I looked at each other and suppressed a giggle.

"...kidnap you and harvest your organs."

"Codpiece! Maggot! Foot licker!"

Hmm, when to interrupt? The air was incredibly tense. I waited for an opening, but the game rolled on. It was as if they were deciding the fate of a real country instead of a land of blood elves, thrones, and halflings. Felix kept touching something under the table.

I tried to get up the nerve to approach him. Before today, my contact with Felix had been limited to grunted hellos in Mathletes. When he spoke, he rarely looked at you and was capable of letting twenty seconds go by before answering a question. "Wish me luck," I whispered to Selfie, and came out from behind the computer terminal.

"Excuse me." I tried to get Felix's attention. "Hi."

Something registered on his face, but he kept on playing. "Fifty groth for the Orthian Plains," he announced.

"Uh . . . Felix?" I cleared my throat.

This time, the other guys looked up.

"Felix!" I burst out.

"You already said that," he noted, without taking his eyes off the dice.

"Well—I didn't know if you heard me." My palms were sweating. "Sorry to interrupt. Can I . . . can I talk to you alone for a minute?"

"Speak quickly. I am aching to destroy you," he said, and everyone laughed. My face felt hot.

"It's a comic book quote," someone explained.

I wiped my brow. These guys made the "cool" table look warm and welcoming. I remembered Roxxi guarding her cafeteria turf like a nightclub bouncer. Who knew a group of nerds could be just as impenetrable?

"Can I drink from the silver goblet?" someone said.

"Affirmative," said Felix. "If *I* can buy the Desert of Qrog."

Being ignored drove me crazy. It was time to bring in the big guns. I could see Selfie crouching behind the computer terminal, awaiting instructions. I motioned for her to come out.

Wearing enough mascara for a *Vogue* cover shoot, Selfie stormed the table. Tossing back her long blond hair, she flashed everyone a dazzling smile. Four faces stared at her, astonished. She planted herself next to them, batting her long eyelashes and awaiting an introduction. None came. "You must be Felix," she said excitedly.

The table went silent.

Had a girl as gorgeous and popular as Selfie ever talked to them before? Had *any* girl? Felix looked stunned, like some fantastical female comic book creature had suddenly come to life. We had their attention now—or at least, Selfie did.

"Can we borrow you for a sec?" Her voice was low and throaty, as though she and Felix were alone. She pointed to a table nearby. "It won't take long. *Please*."

Still staring at Selfie, Felix didn't budge.

"Alone," I added.

Felix's friends nudged him. "Go talk to her, man."

"Yeah, don't be a moron," another said.

Like a zombie, Felix followed us to an empty table. While Prezbo had reacted to Selfie by becoming an insufferable motormouth, Felix had the opposite reaction. He looked positively dazed.

I parked him at the table, facing Selfie and me. He brought his massive backpack with him, dragging it across the carpet. Clutching the strap like a dog leash, he kept staring at Selfie.

"Listen, Felix," I whispered. "We heard about your big prank today."

Felix shifted his stare from Selfie to me. "What prank?"

"Don't play innocent," Selfie hissed.

I smiled grimly. "Better come clean. Unless you want to tell your story down at the principal's office, and I don't think she'd be too happy to hear it." Why was I talking like a guy in a 1940s detective movie? *Sending the principal's bra up a flagpole is an 802, kid. You could do time.*

Felix frowned and stared. Finally, he broke his silence. "Come clean...? About *what*?"

"Just doing it's bad enough," I kept going. "But broadcasting it school-wide? That's beyond mean. That's evil."

"Betrayer!" Selfie spat out. "Disrespecter!"

"Creep!" I piled on. "Bully!"

Felix covered his head like bullets were flying. He started imitating an alarm. "Bleep. Bleep. SYSTEM ERROR. Code not recognized."

"HUH?" Selfie and I both leaned forward. The guy was weird.

"I mean..." Felix started talking in a robot voice. *"What. Are. You. Talking. About?"*

Selfie and I both sighed.

"Does the name 'Rob Robson' ring a bell?" I asked sarcastically.

Felix shifted his stare to the ceiling, as if fascinated by the tile pattern. "He's an eighth grader. I don't know him."

"Yeah." I snorted. "Right."

"I don't know him." His voice was stubborn.

His denials were starting to make me nervous. Droplets of sweat rolled down my neck. He didn't seem capable of having a normal conversation, much less lying. "Then why was your hat in his office?"

"How do I know? I just donated a bag of them to the clothing drive." Felix played with his watch.

"I remember." Selfie nodded. "Along with X-Men socks."

Panic made my head throb. I leaned over the table and got into Felix's face.

"Look, Felix." My voice was short. "We have intel that the biggest prank in school history's about to happen. You've been itching to get in the game. *Did you or did you not* try to sell the school on Craigslist?"

"Affirmative." Felix shrugged. "But what does that have to do with . . . whatever's going on today?"

"Well—"

"I did the Craigslist thing to blow off steam." He pressed more buttons on his watch. "I've been so cratered working on my state science fair project—a robot made of Legos that does chores for senior citizens—I've barely had time to wipe my butt. Much less mastermind some superprank."

Selfie and I looked at each other.

"Senior citizens?" I swallowed.

"Yeah. I'm working with a nursing home to get the commands right. Those people need *help*." Felix had removed his watch and was now taking it apart.

I rubbed my forehead. How could Prezbo have gotten this so wrong? The guy wasn't an evil genius trying to bring down Dr. Valentine—just a comic-book-and-RPG-addled science nerd buried in Legos and software. Who was helping *old people*!

We'd gotten the wrong guy.

"So." I turned again to Felix wearily. "You *really* don't know anything about this big prank today? The broadcast, the flagpole—any of it?"

"Negatory." Felix shook his head. "Craigslist was a solo op, like hacking. Big, coordinated events with other humans? Not my wheelhouse. But I'm flattered by the mistake." He suddenly looked shy.

His gratitude for being accused of a crime was weirdly touching. Nerds didn't have it easy at this school. I felt for him.

"Can I go back to killing blood elves?" He sighed.

"Sure." What a big, fat bust. *Stupid Prezbo!* I motioned to Selfie it was time to go. Getting up from the table, I mistakenly kicked Felix's backpack into the aisle. I stooped to hand it to him. But as soon as I touched the strap, his hand clamped my wrist like a metal claw.

"WHAT ARE YOU DOING?" Felix's eyes were blazing.

"I'm . . ." I was too stunned to speak.

He lunged at me like an angry bull, tackling the backpack as we both fell to the floor. Grunting and flailing, he tried to wrestle it away from me. Instinctively, I clenched the backpack even tighter. What could be inside? When his glasses slipped off, I looked into his eyes and saw . . .

Absolute freaking panic.

"Fight! Fight!" people around us yelled hopefully.

"UNH!" With one final yank, he wrenched the backpack out of my arms and fell onto his back. Something was very, very wrong. And suddenly I knew exactly what was in that backpack.

"What the . . . What in the world is going on here? Get up, Felix!" Mrs. Kavanaugh marched over to us and saw me splayed on the floor. "And who are *you*?"

I scrambled to my feet and jumped next to Selfie.

"I'm Becca; she's Selfie. We're from student council," I said. "We came to ask Felix a technology question."

SHE'S in student council? You could see people thinking as they looked at Selfie. *Where do I sign up?*

Mrs. Kavanaugh frowned and looked down at her clipboard. "Fights will *not* be tolerated. And classroom visitors are required to report directly to me. Is that understood?"

Selfie and I nodded.

Kavanaugh turned to Felix. "And I'm very surprised at your behavior, Felix. Especially after I agreed to let you leave class early today as a favor because you had something going on at lunch."

Felix looked at me and swallowed.

AHA!

Kavanaugh turned back to me. "Did you get your question answered, dear?"

I smiled. "Absolutely."

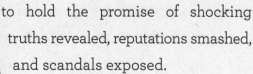

Chapter 11

The crowd on the school lawn stretched all the way to the street. It seemed like every kid at Garfield was sitting on the grass, waiting for the show to begin. Some students were watching on their classrooms' closed-circuit TV. The words *live broadcast* seemed to hold the promise of shocking truths revealed, reputations smashed, and scandals exposed.

The flyers Rob had put out were vague but tantalizing.

"Hey, everyone." Rob took the mic, smiling and pointing to

people in the crowd, like a politician. "We're almost ready. Thanks for chilling while we deal with tech stuff." He and his camera crew were on the lawn, fiddling with tripods, lights, and speakers.

Prezbo and I watched Rob from the school entrance as we waited for Selfie. "How did Rob get permission for this broadcast?" I shook my head. "If they'd known what he was up to, they'd never have let him do it."

"You see Mr. Kurtides?" Prezbo pointed to the journalism teacher and *Action News* adviser standing nearby. "He's keeping an eye on things. Rob will pretend to do an exposé on some sleazy but legit topic— like the rise in obscene graffiti or the 'controversy' over belly button piercing. Then there'll be a commotion nearby, and Rob will be ready with his camera to capture 'breaking news.' That's what happened with the toilet explosion and the french fry fight."

"This time," Prezbo said, "Rob will start his 'top secret' story, and Felix will run out and do his business at the flagpole. And Rob will be right there to broadcast it live. What a scam."

I looked around for Rosa. Remembering our

awkward girls' bathroom encounter made me sad. *If only I had gotten to tell her what happened!* She belonged up here with us, cracking jokes. Would she forgive my behavior when she learned about the Selfie drama? I felt a knot in my throat.

"There's Selfie!" I pointed. The Queen Bee walked toward us as fast as three-inch heels allowed. She was clutching something bulky under her arm. When she got up to Prezbo and me, she put it on her head. "How do I look?"

Prezbo gulped. "Like someone standing in line for a midnight video game release."

In other words, *perfect.*

"Can we just go over the script again?" Selfie bit her lip. "You know, to double-check everything." I could tell she was a little nervous. And why not? She was our last—and *only*—hope of stopping the prank.

"Sure." I pulled out my notes. "Felix hasn't shown up yet."

Selfie read an index card and repeated words to herself. "CGI enhancements ruined *Star Trek*—"

"*Star Wars,*" corrected Prezbo.

"Right." Selfie swallowed. "Aquagirl can't marry a man without gills. Dr. No drowned in a vat of reactor coolant."

"Don't worry about being an expert," I said. "Ask *his* opinions. Who'd beat who in a fight—Wolverine or Batman?"

"Or start a book-versus-movie debate," Prezbo interrupted. "*Harry Potter, Lord of the Rings, Charlie and the Chocolate Factory.*"

Selfie sighed. "This isn't my first time learning stuff for guys. But usually it's, like, names of race car drivers or NBA point guards." I hoped there was still some room in her brain.

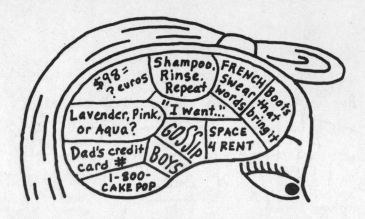

"Just stick to the script," I assured her. But I was nervous, too. "And don't forget to do, you know, the other stuff. Eyelash batting. Hair tossing. Whatever you do." *Was I really telling* Selfie *how to flirt?*

"Girlfriend." She put her hand on her hip and leaned down to meet me at eye level. "I got this."

Despite my nervousness, a little thrill snaked up my neck at "girlfriend."

Suddenly, my nostrils were attacked by expensive French perfume. I turned around and saw Roxxi, Vivienne, and D'Nise standing next to us. *CRUD!* Prezbo gave me an *I'm outta here* look and moved away.

No, no, no, I pleaded silently. *Not now.*

"Ready for the broadcast?" Roxxi smirked. She got closer to Selfie and stared at her outfit. "WHAT are you WEARING!?"

"Nothing." Selfie quickly took off her hat.

"Girl, you better fire your personal shopper," D'Nise said, looking pointedly at me. The other two laughed. "Where are you getting fashion advice—*Computer Weekly*?"

More laughs. Selfie opened her mouth, as if wanting to explain, but closed it again.

Roxxi frowned at Selfie. "Why aren't you sitting where you belong?" She pointed to a section of the lawn that Chaz, Margaux, and Brooklyn had staked out. They seemed to be having a great time. When Roxxi, D'Nise, and Vivienne returned, it would be even more fabulous. How did they manage to make even a scrubby patch of grass look hard to get into?

"And what's the deal with the outfit?" Roxxi's eyes narrowed at Selfie. *"Seriously?"*

Selfie blew a kiss to her friends on the lawn and turned back to Roxxi. *"Chill,* people. The only reason I'm dressed this way is—"

"Got to go! Sorry!" I grabbed Selfie's good arm and tore her away from Roxxi, Vivienne, and D'Nise. I dragged her to another section of the lawn before she could spill about Operation Underwire.

"Talk about *rude!*" Roxxi huffed behind us.

Prezbo ran up to Selfie and me. "I can't find Felix anywhere." He turned to Selfie. "That means that when he appears, you'll have to grab him on his way to the flagpole. Try to work fast because the walk will only take a minute. Ninety seconds, max. Ready?"

Selfie nodded, while I did a run-through of the props Selfie was supposed to have with her:

"Frozen syrup drink in Slurptastic Strawberry?"

"Check."

"Twenty-sided dice?"

"Yep."

"*Star Wars* candy?"

"Got 'em."

I knew I'd overprepared, but that was what I always did—whether studying for a debate championship or taking a *Girls' World* magazine quiz. I couldn't leave anything to chance.

"Two seconds, people!" Rob grabbed the mic again.

With time running out, Prezbo and I whispered last-minute instructions to Selfie.

"Wear glasses!"

"*Don't* wear glasses!"

"Mention 'hyper-speed'!"

"Offer exploding gum!"

"And if nothing works? Here's your nuclear option." Prezbo's voice got low and serious. "Ask for his *top ten lists*: Best Shark Movies. Fakest Wrestlers. Lamest Sequels."

"What if he doesn't have any?" asked Selfie.

" 'Course he's got 'em." Prezbo snorted. "What do you think nerds do all day?"

"Good. Got it. Now I need space." Selfie covered her ears. She took deep breaths, like a Broadway star before opening night. "Don't worry, guys. I'm going to *destroy* out there. If I need to, I'll make stuff up."

"DON'T DO THAT!!" Prezbo and I both shouted at once.

Rob's voice boomed again. "And now, the moment you've all been waiting for. This is Rob Robson with a special *Action News* live broadcast."

This is it, I thought. *The last chance to save ourselves!*

My heart was beating crazily. I whispered to Selfie and Prezbo. "Let's all get in position." Selfie planted herself near the school entrance as the last stragglers rushed to find a spot on the lawn. Prezbo and I stood close enough to be within earshot, our faces as blank as Secret Service men's.

"Today we bring you a story so putrid, so vile, so disgusting . . ." Rob went into grim anchorperson mode. "People with weak stomachs are advised not to watch. We're serious. If you're the least bit prone to hurling . . ."

Now he had our attention. The crowd became deadly silent as they leaned forward, riveted by all the revolting possibilities.

"Please excuse yourself. Because today's subject is ... dog poop."

A round of *Ewwwwwwws*.

"This school has a dog poop crisis. Every day, piles of poop get dumped on the school lawn. You could be sitting in some right now...."

"Ick! Gross!" the crowd squealed, checking the ground beneath them.

"Dog poop contains hookworms, tapeworms, and other really foul stuff. It can contaminate the water supply and soil. What most people don't know is ... *dog poop is a silent killer.*"

Prezbo and I broke from bodyguard stance to roll our eyes. In RobWorld, everything was a "crisis" or a "killer." He was always trying to stir up shock and fear and feed our appetite for gory details. Today's story was probably especially bogus because he didn't have to finish it; at any moment, he was going to interrupt for "breaking news." I looked around for Felix but didn't see him anywhere.

"Lately, things have gotten out of control. People are letting dog poop pile up—" Rob's eyes darted to the school entrance, and his voice got louder. "I *said,* people are letting DOG POOP PILE UP...."

Someone had missed their cue. Rob looked nervously at the entrance again.

"People are letting *dog poop pile up*...." Rob cleared his throat and waited. Nothing happened.

Prezbo and I exchanged glances. Where was Felix?

Rob wiped his forehead. "Think about it. The average dog has to do number two maybe twice a day, which adds up to ... um ... fourteen piles of poop in one week. And that's just *one* dog—" He was babbling.

The audience looked baffled. As Rob jabbered on, his report got weirder and weirder. "Of course, the amount of poop varies from dog to dog. I mean, Great Danes, right? I bet they drop a *monster* load of—"

"Get to the point, Rob," Mr. Kurtides, the journalism teacher, interrupted from the lawn.

People started getting restless, snapping gum and thumb wrestling.

"Boooo!" someone started, and others picked it up. "BOOOO!" They'd been lured to the lawn with the promise of a juicy, tabloid-style exposé, and he was giving them . . . *dog poop.*

Something rustled behind us. I turned around—nothing. Then I heard it again. Was it coming from the shrubbery? I leaned back and noticed a baseball hat rising from the bushes.

It was Felix! I nudged Selfie, and she tiptoed over to him. He stood up slowly, clutching his backpack and looking around uncertainly.

"There you are!" Selfie grabbed his arm.

He leaped back, startled.

"Sorry we cratered your *ScepterQuest* game this morning." Selfie flashed her dazzling smile. "When I'm not in Fashion Club, I'm a level eighty-five blood elf. (Shhh, don't tell anyone!) Want to share buttered-popcorn-flavored jelly beans with me—food of the gods!—and watch *Die, Cyclops, Die!*? The 1961 original, not the super-lame remake."

Felix's mouth dropped.

Selfie put out her good arm. "Can you help me to my locker? Stupid cast! I got bonked in the *Zombie Sharks* opening-day ticket line. Now I have to read comic books with one hand."

Felix's eyes got huge, like he was about to explode. It was probably the most female attention he'd ever gotten! And from a drop-dead gorgeous gamer with an oozing eyeball tattoo!

Her arm remained in the air, smart watch flickering like

an invitation. "Oh, and remind me to show you this video. A dog riding a tortoise—it's insane." She took a snack package out of her pocket. "Chocolate-dipped Oreo?"

Felix gasped.

OREOS? Plus cult films, comics, a beautiful blond? This was, like, his craziest dream come true! *What guy could resist?*

Looking confused, he gave her his arm.

YES!!!

Contact achieved. As he reached out to her, his other shoulder went slack, and his backpack dropped. I dove for it.

Easing down the zipper, I reached in and felt lace and curving underwire. A second later, the bra was in my hand. Victory!

God, the thing was huge. I tried to hide it under my arms. Felix spun around and tried to grab it back, but it was too late. I shot off like a rocket.

Robson pointed to me and yelled, "GET HER!" His goons came after me like angry hornets as I flew across the lawn. Who knew I could run so fast? The whole school gaped as their hotshot news anchor totally lost it.

Mr. Kurtides yelled for everyone to stay seated. The audience obeyed, riveted by the drama—except for one person. Someone was jumping up and down like an angry sports fan. I turned to see the tantrum thrower.

It was Roxxi.

That's weird, I thought. *What is she so mad about?*

Looking behind me, I saw Rob and Felix had joined the chase. "Rob. ROB! What about the broadcast?" a frazzled Kurtides called after him.

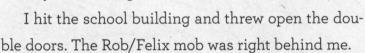

As I flew by Prezbo, he slapped my back. Selfie yelled, "Go, girl!"

I hit the school building and threw open the double doors. The Rob/Felix mob was right behind me.

Inside, a teacher stared. I sailed by her. She shouted after me, "Young lady! STOP! Did you hear me? YOUNG LADY!"

Where to go? I stood at the intersection of two empty halls on the main floor, gasping for breath. Hiding was impossible. In two seconds, I'd be sixth-grade roadkill.

Behind me were *guys*. Older, eighth-grade guys. Guys who hated me for spoiling a once-in-a-lifetime prank.

"THERE SHE IS!" they shouted from down the hall. *Crud!*

Should I bust into a classroom? Hit the cafeteria? Go straight to the principal? No, not with these jerks on my back. Then it hit me like a thunderbolt. Lurching forward, I sprinted to the ONE place they couldn't enter....

Opening the door, I pulled it tight behind me and flung the bra onto a counter. I was inside—*PHEW!* They wouldn't dare come in. A half second later, I heard them crash against the door.

POUND! POUND! POUND!

"Get your butt out here!" Rob yelled.

"We'll break the freakin' door down!" someone screamed.

"What I cannot have, I will destroy!" That was Felix.

"YOU'RE DEAD!" Rob growled.

Looking around the bathroom, my heart sank. *No window!* The only way out was back through that door, where an angry mob waited to behead me.

I picked up the bra from the counter, hooking my thumbs around the straps. For the first time, I got a good look. It was an amazing piece of architecture, with elaborate supports, latches, and bows—as indestructible as the Brooklyn Bridge. I stretched it out and looked at it upside down.

I was holding the principal's bra.

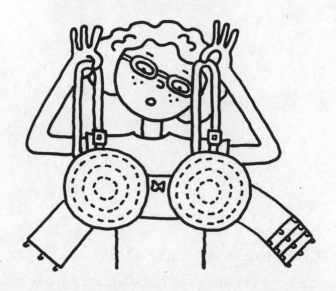

POUND! POUND! POUND!

Why had I thought I was safe here? I probably had two seconds left before they burst through the door. I had to hide the bra—but *where*? I'd left my backpack with Prezbo, and my pants didn't have pockets. If they saw the bra in my hand, they'd grab it.

There was nothing to do but ... (gulp) ...

Wear it.

Chapter 12

*W*hoa.

The sight of myself in a DDD bra made me gasp. It was so large I could have fit two more people inside. Shortening the straps didn't help. What a contrast to what I usually wore.

I'd always wondered how I'd look with a bust. Slipping my T-shirt back on, I examined myself in the

mirror. Instead of cute curves, there seemed to be some hard-to-identify object up my shirt. I looked idiotic.

POUND! POUND! POUND!

No way could I walk around like this. I needed a jacket to hide my weird shape. But with Rob's goons outside, there was no way to get to my locker. Now the door was opening. . . .

Holy crud!

"Where is it? WHERE IS IT?" Rob pushed me aside, panting. At least ten guys rushed in, falling over themselves like the Three Stooges. They poured into every corner of the bathroom, searching frantically.

"I don't know." I folded my arms across my chest.

"Liar." Rob's voice burned with anger as he backed me against the wall. I kept my arms in front of me. "We saw you steal it. Well, it's a hot news story, and we're covering it—no matter what."

"'News' story, Rob?" I shot back. "You're helping with the prank! That's *creating* the news—not covering it. It's fake journalism. And it's REALLY MEAN!"

"Thief!" he spat out.

"Sleazebag!" I hurled back.

I leaped for the door, still covering my chest. But Rob jumped up to block me. "No way. You're not going *anywhere*."

Rob turned back to his troops and barked out orders. "See if you can find her purse, backpack, jacket—*anything*. Check every container and wastebasket. It's here somewhere."

Felix just stood there.

"GO!" Rob yelled, making him jump.

Awkwardly, I stood frozen against the wall, trying to hide the bulge under my shirt. One of Rob's buddies, the short guy with glasses, was ordered to stand guard near the door. His eyes kept straying to my chest. I hugged myself to block his view.

Meanwhile, Rob's crew scoured the room like detectives at a crime scene. "What the ...?" One of the guys stopped and looked at the writing on the wall. "What *is* this?"

Another guy came over.

"Hottie List," he read aloud.

That got everyone's attention. "*Hottie List?*" "Huh!" "Where?" Pretty soon, all the guys were gathered around, squinting at the wall. For a moment, they read silently. Then they all talked at once.

"Ajax, NUMBER ONE? *No way.*"

"Who's Dinesh O'Reilly?"

"*Puh*-lease!"

"Belasco—"

"Who WROTE this?"

Rob stomped over, furious. "What are you morons doing? We've got work to do. GET AWAY FROM THAT FREAKIN' WALL!" Rob's eyes skimmed the list. "Hoberman's *fourth*? That's bogus."

While the guys were distracted, I edged toward the door, little by little. Suddenly the door crashed open again, and I heard an adult voice.

"What—WHAT—is going on . . . ?"

Ms. Wandelmeyer, a tall science teacher with ferocious eyebrows, stood at the open door. Behind her, students in the hall stared. Rob's guys gasped and jumped back. Rob started sputtering.

"A student reported she couldn't get into the bathroom." Wandelmeyer shook her head as she strode into the sea of pink tile. "Now I see why! What in the WORLD are you boys doing in here?"

"We were, uh, looking for, uh, something. . . ." He fell silent, perhaps realizing explanations were impossible. Wandelmeyer waited. When Rob's words trailed off, she pressed him into a corner.

"*Yes,* Mr. Robson? What WERE you looking for?"

Her eyebrows tilted up like Nike swooshes. "I'd very much like to know."

This was my big chance. I tiptoed toward the door and slipped out. *Freedom!*

Relief washed over me . . . until I looked at my watch and freaked out. It was twelve fifty-five. The principal had arrived ten minutes ago.

• • ● • •

Run. Run. Run.

I begged my legs to go faster as they bolted to the principal's office. There was no time to find Selfie. I sped past a couple of sixth-grade girls, barely seeing them. A second later I heard giggling.

Crud! I'd forgotten about the lumps under my shirt! Girls would *definitely* notice. The Bust

Development Race was highly competitive; we were always sneaking looks in the locker room to see who had filled out. I was practically last in my grade to experience the miraculous changes described in the health-class film.

I stopped to catch my breath, resting my hands on my knees. Forgetting to hide my chest, I stretched out for a moment. *You can't afford to rest*, I told myself. *Run! Run! Run!*

"Yo."

Ajax Webber, the school bully, blocked my way. His two friends, Scab and B.B., circled like buzzards. The bullies had never come up to me before. What was going on?

"How's that Hottie List?" He stared at my chest.

"All set." I panted. "Sorry, I have to—"

"What's the rush?" Ajax smiled lazily.

"Skittle?" Scab held out a bag of candy as his eyes traveled down my shirt.

Geez! Were these guys seriously just . . . openly gawking? My stomach fluttered wildly. For the first time, I had sympathy for big-busted girls. Usually their "complaints" annoyed me—they had backaches, popped buttons, trouble finding bathing suits. Guys stared at them when the word *mountain* came up in class. Now I felt their pain.

"Eyes up here!" I barked. *Words I'd never said before.*

"Huh?" Ajax seemed startled.

Since when had I become a guy magnet? Ajax and

his friends usually went for tough-looking girls with clumpy mascara. Now all three were grinning like morons.

"Becca?"

I looked up and saw Rosa. I couldn't believe it! Oh, that was perfect. Just perfect. Really, this day couldn't get any better. Her eyes widened as they dipped below my neck. If she thought I'd turned into an airhead before, what would she think now that I had *fake boobs*?

"Get lost," Rosa snarled to the bullies.

Pulling me aside, Rosa eyed my chest and shook her head sadly. "It's like I don't even know you anymore."

Her words hit me like a punch in the gut—*but I had to get to Valentine.* "Rosa, I've got to run, but I'll explain later! Promise!" I begged.

Rosa watched me bolt. This time I wasn't stopping—for anyone. *Don't open the bag*, I silently begged Valentine. *Two seconds and I'll be there!*

I zoomed down the corridor, soaring through the halls.

Turning in to the maze of administration offices, I slammed into someone. "Ow!" My arm hit something hard. I sprang back and saw a whirl of blond hair.

"Selfie?" I rubbed my arm.

"Becca!" She waved her cast. "I've been looking all over for you!"

"We've got to—" I pointed to the principal's office.

"Totally!" She squinted at my chest and frowned. "Hey, what have you got under your—"

Not again. Please not again.

"I think you know," I said quietly.

Selfie's voice became sympathetic. "Look, you want to look more grown-up—I get it. But I don't think—"

"I'm NOT trying to look grown-up!" I whispered fiercely.

"Then why—"

I pulled Selfie aside. Lifting up my T-shirt for a second, I flashed my new undergarment.

Selfie's eyes widened. "NOOOOOO!"

"*Yes.*" I pulled down the shirt. "Now GO! We're late!"

We shot off toward the office, sprinting until we hit Maslon's cubicle. When we saw the door, we gasped. We were too late! She was already there.

"We need . . . to see . . . the principal." I panted.

"Principal, yeah." Selfie was panting, too.

Mr. Maslon was calmly thumbing through *World of Antiques* magazine and sipping a mug of tea. "Sorry. She's not seeing students until three—"

"We can't wait that long," I interrupted.

"It's an emergency," added Selfie. "*Mega.* Not just like, 'My purse strap broke' or 'I have to miss gym.'"

"Oh, it's *you.*" Maslon peered over his glasses. "The ones who—"

Heat rose up my neck. "Listen, we just need to see her for a minute. *Less* than a minute."

"What's this about?" Maslon frowned.

We need to slip the principal's bra back into her shopping bag before she notices it's missing. "It's a female thing." I looked at the floor to hint at some kind of urgent-but-too-private-to-discuss emergency. Usually "female things" were a Get Out of Jail Free Card that made guys blush and give you anything you wanted. But Maslon was no pushover.

"Gym excuse, nurse pass, or feminine supplies?" His voice was bored.

Dr. Valentine could be opening the bag this very minute! Couldn't he give us a freakin' break?

"Mr. Maslon—" My heart pounded. "We need to get in there. Can you just ask her?"

"Ladies, I don't make the rules," Maslon said briskly. "If I did, this drink would be a martini, and these shoes would be slipper socks."

"Can't you just—" I started.

"Dr. Valentine just got back to her office. She's tied up all day with *very important* school business."

"Mr. Maslon." Dr. Valentine's voice blared out of the speakerphone next to him. "I need an opinion. Do you think I can wear the white dance outfit with red cowboy boots?"

Maslon grabbed the receiver and turned away from us. "The one with the rhinestones?" he whispered.

Ha! Selfie and I pretended not to hear. I played with a London snow globe on his desk.

"Let me just show you—" Dr. Valentine said as she burst through the door in a cloud of sweet perfume.

We jumped back, startled. Maslon fumbled with the phone. When Valentine saw Selfie and me, she frowned.

"Well, well, well." Dr. Valentine folded the shirt over her arm and looked down at us through half glasses. "I'm not surprised to see the two of you back at my office."

Selfie and I gulped. What did that mean? *Had she noticed her shopping bag had no bra in it?*

Maslon looked agitated. "I told them you weren't seeing students—"

"I'll handle it, Mr. Maslon." She gestured for us to follow her into her office. "You may come in."

The minute I entered the room, my eyes located the shopping bag. It was on one of the cabinets, next to some dance trophies.

Dr. Valentine hung the shirt on a coatrack and sat down. Leaning back in her chair, she stared at us in silence.

"Well . . . ?" Valentine frowned.

Selfie looked at me. I looked at Selfie. *Did Valentine know about the missing bra?*

"What did you do *this* time?" Valentine leaned across her desk. "Skip gym and go to a shoe sale? Sneak into a high school dance? Arrest a sixth grader for 'fashion crimes'?"

Joy surged through me. She didn't know the bra was missing! *She didn't know the bra was missing!* It was too good to be true. Being accused of multiple wrongs had never felt so good.

Now the hard part.

Could I unhook the bra and slip it into the shopping bag? If she looked away for a minute, it was maybe—*maybe*—possible. Trying was sheer insanity, but I was desperate. My mind groped for ways to distract her.

"We didn't do any of those things!" Selfie protested, offended by the principal's accusations. I kicked her under the chair. Valentine's insults didn't matter; we needed to prolong the meeting. That way, when she eventually turned her back, I could sneak over to the bag and slip the bra in.

"The reason we're here is . . ." I stalled. *Think of something—anything!* "We wanted to know if spaghetti straps are acceptable on prom dresses. Because according to paragraph 321a of the school bylaws,

'Strapless gowns on prom night are illegal and unlawful.' Message received. But do teeny-tiny spaghetti straps the width of gift ribbon violate the rule? We need, uh, clarification."

Valentine stared, speechless.

"Spaghetti straps." Her voice was flat. "You came to the principal's office to discuss . . . *spaghetti straps*?"

Selfie nodded enthusiastically. Now, *this* was a subject she could get into! "Yes." She lifted her chin. "Sure, it's early to be thinking about prom, but the good shopping sites suggest a six-month lead time. I mean, it's the biggest night of your life, right? Aside from the Fashion Club Black-and-White Ball, Teen Cotillion, Junior Chicago Fire and Ice, and Country Club Casino Night."

Valentine shook her head. "I don't believe this. I really do not believe this." She sighed heavily. "You want me to check the *bylaws*?"

"If it's not too much trouble." I nodded. *Score!*

Valentine spun her rolling chair around and opened a file cabinet behind her desk, snorting. "Spaghetti straps. And I thought I'd heard it *all*."

MY BIG CHANCE!

With Valentine's back turned, I reached under my shirt, looking for the clasp. *Crud!* It wouldn't unhook! I had to try from a better angle. Frantically, I started to pull my shirt off. Now my arms were above my head, stuck in my shirt.

"These 'bylaws' you mentioned." Valentine turned slightly, so we saw her head in profile. "I can't find them. Are you sure you're not talking about the School Constitution?"

"Ummph unh Pffmb." I tried to speak.

"Ex*cuse* me?" Valentine sighed.

I pulled my head back through the neck hole. "Maybe it *was* the constitution. Or rules & regulations. Paragraph 321a. Or 231b. Something like that."

Valentine turned back to the file cabinet, and I tried to pull the shirt over my head again. Maybe if I twisted it around . . .

"Becca—" Selfie's whisper held a warning.

The shirt was still tangled up above my head, while the enormous bra dangled from my shoulders. Finally, I got the clasp unhooked—*YES!* I yanked the shirt back down. Now if I could just pull the bra up through the neck hole—

That's when the principal turned around.

"Ms. Birnbaum." The principal's eyes widened, and then she stood up. "Are you . . . *wearing my bra*?"

Chapter 13

"I can explain!" I gasped, wrenching the bra off. I laid it on the edge of her desk.

Valentine blinked and blinked again. She looked like she was in shock. Without taking her eyes off me, she reached for the bra and placed it in a desk drawer.

It was—*without a doubt*—the worst moment of my life.

Valentine sat down, her face frozen. She said something, but I didn't hear it. My heart was beating too loud.

"Sorry—what did you say?" My voice came out strangled. I glanced at Selfie, who looked too terrified to breathe.

"I said..." The principal's tone was icy. "*I'm waiting.*"

What freaked me out most was how Valentine didn't seem exactly angry. She was more... *astounded.* Even a seen-it-all, heard-it-all old schooler like her couldn't believe her eyes. We were all in completely new territory.

And that was *way* scarier.

"Okay." Deep breath.

Silence.

Selfie's eyes begged me not to rat her out. But the truth was, *I had no idea what I was going to say.*

"It all started when I came to pick up Selfie's shopping bag." I tried to steady my voice. "And I took the wrong one, by mistake."

Selfie's body stiffened.

"We wanted to return the, uh, item, immediately. But it fell into the hands of some shady characters." I looked down at my feet.

Valentine picked up a pencil and started writing on a legal pad.

"Mr. Maslon spotted Selfie with the empty shopping bag and grabbed it out of her hand, not realizing it was empty. He put it back in your office." I pointed to the bag.

"And then . . . ?"

"We heard this, uh, bra-jacker was going public. *Very* public."

"We were worried out of our minds—seriously! Then, just as the whole insane thing was about to go viral . . ." My throat clenched as I remembered our last-minute save. "I stole it back."

Valentine swallowed. But her pencil kept moving. "The bad guy and his friends were chasing me, but I didn't have a backpack or anything to put it in. There was only ONE safe way to transport it...."

Valentine tightened her lips.

"And that's how I ended up..." I swallowed. "In your bra."

Words I never expected to say to a principal.

Selfie looked grateful that I hadn't pinned it all on her. Her eyes said, *Good try,* but we both knew we were doomed. The only noise in the room was the sound of Valentine's pencil moving furiously across the page. *Scratch scratch scratch.*

And then the noise stopped.

Silence.

I dared to look at Dr. Valentine. She had put down the pencil and was sitting perfectly still, her face blank, arms folded, eyes staring straight ahead.

Selfie and I held our breath.

Did she believe me?

The answer could destroy us.

What would my parents say?

Thinking about them getting a call from the principal filled me with a heavy heart. Hadn't they sacrificed to give me every opportunity? My dad always said proudly, "Some parents don't trust their kids. But we never have to worry about you. You always do the right thing."

Oh, Dad, I thought sadly. *I'm so sorry.*

I wondered if I'd have to change schools, too.

It was the kind of moment that divided your life in two. Until now, I hadn't realized how good I'd had it. Random scenes flashed through my mind: eating lunch with Rosa and Prezbo, curling up with a

book, winning second place in a creative-writing contest, the thrill of meeting Selfie. My old life, with its little pleasures and disappointments, suddenly looked amazing. Why hadn't I appreciated it?

Now our future hinged on Valentine believing a vague, rambling tale that barely added up. I looked over at Selfie, who was glumly turning a bangle bracelet. We looked at each other in despair.

Valentine was still staring.

Why was she torturing us? The silence was excruciating. *Go ahead and lose it already—yell! Scream! Flip out! Tell us how deeply disappointed you are. Say you feel personally betrayed. Rant about our moral failings. Just . . . say . . .* something!

Valentine cleared her throat. Selfie and I sat up straight. Was she finally going to speak?

"Ms. Birnbaum, Ms. St. Clair." She pressed her lips together.

Selfie and I leaned forward.

"I don't think that's the whole story," Valentine said quietly.

Both of us swallowed.

Valentine's eyebrows drew together as she leaned forward impatiently. "Who are these quote unquote 'shady characters'? How did the item fall into their hands? Why were they looking for you? These are *basic questions.*"

Selfie and I looked at each other in terror. Of course, Valentine wanted specifics! Now we were sunk. I gripped the armrest of the chair, trying to think of what to say. My legs were like noodles. My stomach felt sick. My mouth tasted sour. What would happen to us?

"I . . . um . . ." My mouth was stuck.

We sat there in miserable silence. Valentine

unfolded her arms and rubbed her forehead. "And
yet—"

We blinked back tears.

"I'm going to let it go." Valentine sighed.

"Huh?" Selfie and I gasped, astonished.

Valentine leaned back in her chair and shook her
head. "I don't want to make you into tattletales. You
got my belongings back to me in a sensitive situation. And for that . . ." Her voice turned husky. "I'm
very grateful."

My brain couldn't quite take it in.

Did that mean—we *weren't* in trouble?

"Can you imagine what might have happened if
this . . . article . . . had gotten out into the school's general population?" Valentine shuddered. "It could have
been . . ."

"The subject of a thousand Instagrams," I dared
to say.

Valentine drew in a deep breath. "That's why details aren't important. What matters is: The garment left this office. You brought it back." The principal and I locked eyes in a moment of understanding. Her expression said she knew the incident had had the potential to become a legendary, school-wide, principal-shaming fiasco—and it hadn't. *Thanks for keeping your mouth shut.*

Dr. Valentine's phone rang. "Yes, Mr. Maslon?" She listened. "That's right. Six o'clock at Denim and Diamonds. It's the regional championships...."

While Dr. Valentine was talking, Selfie squeezed my knee, her face excited.

"No Swiss boarding school!" she whispered. "No sunrise hikes! No French tutor!"

I started to feel giddy, too. We *were* pretty amazing. We had saved the day. Maybe the principal would give us an award. Medal of honor? Trophy? Public recognition? But, of course, she could never say what it was for.

When Dr. Valentine hung up the phone, she saw our lit-up faces and frowned. "Don't be too impressed with yourselves." She wagged her finger. "You're still on thin ice at this school, Ms. St. Clair. And Ms. Birnbaum, being her accomplice is not the path to—"

I didn't hear the rest of the sentence. My eyes were glued to the window, where something white was moving up the flagpole. (Hint: It was *not* the American flag.) Selfie saw it, too, and we traded glances as it climbed higher and higher.

"Ladies. LADIES! I'm talking! Why—?" Valentine turned around and gasped. *"What on God's green earth . . . ?"*

Underpants flapped in the air like the flag of some strange country.

She leaped up and grabbed the phone. "Mr. Maslon? Mr. Maslon? Have you looked out the window? Of all the foolishness . . ."

While she was barking orders, we ran over to the window. Looking down, I spotted Prezbo at the base of the flagpole, pulling the rope. He waved at me through the window and hoisted the underwear to the top. Then he ran.

The bell rang and we slipped away.

· · ● · ·

Selfie and I left Valentine's office in a daze. It was passing period, and the halls were jammed. We flagged down Prezbo, who nearly ran by us, out of breath. "Come here!" I shouted as I pulled him aside. Selfie and I blasted him with questions. "Why were you at the flagpole? Whose underwear was that?" Between gulps of air, he filled us in. We couldn't believe our ears.

"The tighty-whities were *Rob's*?" My mouth fell open.

"GET! OUT!" Selfie pushed Prezbo.

Still panting, Prezbo held up his hand. "Swear."

"How . . . ?"

But Prez wasn't paying attention. His hand was in the air, waving to someone. A couple of seconds later, Rosa came up to us. I felt myself stiffen.

"Hey." Her eyes took in Selfie and me.

Everyone looked at the floor.

I broke the silence. "We were just asking Prezbo," I mumbled, "how he, you know, got Robson's underwear."

Rosa broke into a sly smile.

"Let's just say . . ." Her eyes gleamed. "The clothing drive has some great finds. Lucky for us, Rob's mom sews labels on his camp clothes."

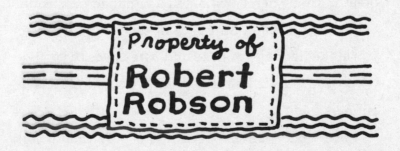

WHAT?

This was *Rosa's* doing? My heart leaped.

"When Prezbo explained *what happened* . . ." Rosa looked at me meaningfully, lingering on the words for emphasis. "I wanted revenge."

"Wow." Selfie looked at her with shining eyes. "That is so sick."

"Stealing Rob's underwear wasn't easy," Rosa added. "Especially with Roxxi working the clothing drive. But she was so busy whispering to Felix Needleman—"

"Felix Needleman!?" I grabbed her arm. "Rosa, did you say . . . *Felix Needleman?*"

"Felix, yeah." Rosa shrugged. "How crazy is that?"

"Holy crud!" I slapped my forehead, looking at everyone. "That's how Felix got the bra! Don't you see? She was at the Fashion Club meeting—"

"When I was bra-napped," Selfie finished.

Remembering Roxxi's angry tantrum at the broadcast, I looked at Selfie and sighed. "If only we could prove it . . ."

Selfie shook her head sadly. "We'll never know the dirty deets. Welcome to my life."

"I thought you guys were friends?" Rosa turned to Selfie, confused.

"*Frenemies*," Selfie corrected. "If she's in full-on beast mode, she'll start a rumor my new bae and I are breaking up. Other times, she'll let me copy the homework *she* copied from someone. So: It's complicated."

Huh? Rosa and I traded smiles at the Selfie-speak. We were okay again.

Prezbo looked at his watch. "I'm going upstairs—"

"Me too." Rosa waved at us. "Want to watch TV later?"

My heart leaped. "YES!"

Now it was just Selfie and me.

"I can't believe how it all turned out." Selfie shook her head again. "The way you handled the principal? You killed it! Who'd ever have thought of . . ." She made a face. "*Telling the truth?*"

I shrugged. "She was just grateful to have it back."

When we got to the main hallway, we both stopped. "I'm going this way . . ."

"I'm headed that way—"

Was this . . . good-bye?

Across the hall, her friends called out to her, "Selfie! SELFIE!" I felt a lump in my throat as they crowded around. "Where've you been, girl? Get over here!" Our time together as fellow warriors was over. I'd go back to allergy shots and biographies of women scientists; she'd go back to high school parties and heli-skiing.

Why was that so disappointing? I'd always known our friendship had a shelf life. But we'd had some

weird and unforgettable moments together. *No one else knew what it was like to be in that room with Dr. Valentine.*

I was really going to miss Selfie. Her ridiculous purse and useless pink feather pen. The diet croissants and three-inch heels. Her nose for trouble and absurd glam life. The way her eyes sparkled when she came up with another terrible idea.

I was also going to miss parts of me that came out when I was with her. The part that was (maybe! a little!) curious about boys. The part that loved coming to the rescue.

Her friends kept chattering.

"You going to Tad's later? His parents are in Bar-
bados—"

"No, come with us! Sisters before misters."

"... clambake at the club—"

I had to let her go.

I forced myself to walk away. Seconds later, I felt a
hand squeeze my arm.

"Becca—wait!"

I spun around. Selfie was in front of me.

"I just wanted to say thanks. *Mega*-thanks," she
said softly. "You rock, even with a triple-D bra around
your neck."

I smiled.

"And I hope we'll still hang out. I think you're ...
you're really cool."

I filed her words away to enjoy later, like the corner of a chocolate bar.

"Oh! And don't worry." She blushed. "You won't need to solve my problems anymore. I think I've really, like, *grown up* from this. I'm more mature."

"Great," I said.

"Selfie!" Her friends were calling.

She smiled again, and D'Nise grabbed her arm. For a moment, she resisted, but then her friends swallowed her up completely, and I couldn't see her anymore.

Walking away, I felt sad. Life was officially back to normal.

Ten minutes later, my phone pinged.

To: Becca
From: Selfie
Can you meet ASAP??!! A teensy major
trauma has come up!!!!!

Here we go, I thought.
I smiled.

Don't miss the unlikely duo's next adventure!

THIS DANCE IS DOOMED

**COMING
SPRING 2019**

mackids.com